Ride With My Heart

My Heart

A Southland Romance

By Meda White

Ride With My Heart
Copyright © 2015 Meda White

Editor: Andrea Grimm Dickinson
Cover Artist: Kari Ayasha, Cover to Cover Designs

ISBN: 1941287107
ISBN-13: 978-1-941287-10-1

DEDICATION

For the survivors—
You're stronger than you know.

To Lori Preston for sharing your love of animals with
me and all the cousins.

In loving memory of Trigger (1968-2000),
the gentle Strawberry roan Tennessee Walker on which
an entire generation of Faircloths learned to ride.

ACKNOWLEDGMENTS

Thank you to my real life team roping friends, Mitchell and Kristin Bass for the inspiration.

Thank you to the Faircloth clan for sharing the stories, including the near death experiences.

Chapter One

Maddie Baker's date morphed into an octopus when the clock struck midnight. Between the tequila and the beer, celebrating her divorce was turning into *Invasion of the Booty Snatcher*.

The roaming hands belonged to hometown boy and former Arena football player, Ricky Dalton. Granted, she should have stopped drinking hours before, but she also should've been safe on the little dance floor at Mason's Jar Bar.

The watering hole was owned and operated by a family friend named Mason, and it was apropos that the beverages, from draft beer to mixed drinks, were served in Mason jars. Having lived so long in Atlanta, Maddie loved the ambiance of the country bar with wooden floors, walls, and bar. The smell of sin, booze, and cigarette smoke permeated the air. A little sawdust on the dance floor and a local band playing southern rock made it a second home for anyone looking for a good time.

Accepting a date with Willow Creek's most eligible bachelor had seemed like a good idea when the final papers arrived in the mail. But by one in the morning, Maddie regretted her decision and her anger toward her ex-husband grew with each grope. It was Mark's fault she was in this position. No woman should have to endure being fondled against her will.

Every time Maddie removed Ricky's hand from her rear end, his other hand snuck down to the other cheek. She should have expected as much from a former receiver.

Gritting her teeth, she put her hands on his chest and pushed. She might as well have tried to push through a brick wall for all the good it did. The son of a bitch chuckled and pulled her closer.

Temporarily trapped in his grip, long-suppressed panic began to surface. Everything she knew to do flew from her buzzed brain. The knowledge returned in a slow motion whirlwind, and just as she'd decided on a course of action, another variable came into play.

"May I cut in?"

Ricky's hands loosened as Maddie looked to see if she had a savior or another horn-dog lookin' to score. Her shoulders sagged as relief flooded her.

"Heath." Her voice pitched higher than normal as she shoved away from Ricky and threw her arms around Heath's neck.

Ricky tugged her arm. "Get lost, guy. The lady is with me."

Ignoring her date, Maddie held on to her old friend's arm for dear life. "I haven't seen you in forever." Really, it had only been a year and a half, but who was counting?

"It has been a little while. I heard you were back in town." Heath squeezed her hand. "How 'bout that dance?"

"Maybe you didn't hear me the first time." Ricky stepped between them. "Maddie is *my* date."

They looked like two linemen squaring off, both massive muscle heads over six feet tall.

Maddie eased between them and put a hand on Ricky's chest. "Don't be jealous of Heath. He's like my brother." She nodded toward the bar. "Now, go get us a couple of shots while I dance with my friend." *Whew. In-charge Maddie was back.*

Ricky narrowed his eyes a split-second before he shrugged and meandered off in the direction of the bar.

Heath moved in and placed his hands on her waist. "I'd say you've had enough to drink."

"I know." She covered her mouth to suppress a burp. "'Scuse me, this inebriation is gonna hurt like hell in the mornin'."

"What are you doing with Ricky Dalton? That guy's a creep, Mad." A tiny crease rested between his brows.

From her position, looking up past his dimple into his ice blue eyes, she wondered if he'd always been so beautiful. The answer was *yes, always, and even more so now.* "I know, right? Pickings are slim in Willow Creek. I wanted to move on, and he asked me out. I swear the man's got ten hands."

"Do you need me to take you home?" Heath asked.

Maddie looked for Ricky at the bar and found him chatting it up with Loose-Lips Linda. *Thank God for small favors.* For a split second, Maddie's manners warred with her good sense. *Screw that.* Politeness got a lot of women in trouble.

"I don't think he'd notice if I disappeared," Maddie said. "I'd appreciate the ride, Heath. I'm definitely safer with you."

"I wouldn't be so sure about that, Maddie-cake. You're unattached, and not a little girl anymore." He wriggled his eyebrows as he looked her over.

She smacked his chest, even as heat surged to places that hadn't been warm in a while. One thing she knew for sure, this man would never, ever hurt her. At least, not on purpose. "You're such a kidder. Come on, let's blow this Mason jar."

***

Heath helped Maddie up into his truck by gripping her waist. As much as he wanted to cop a feel, her butt had been grabbed enough for one night. He'd considered resigning his badge and strangling Ricky Dalton when he couldn't keep his hands to himself. The more Maddie struggled, the more aggressive the bastard had gotten.

Walking around the back of his truck, Heath shook off the anger. If it hadn't been *his* Maddie-cake, he probably wouldn't have noticed. He slid behind the wheel and watched her buckle her seatbelt and then recline the seat. Almost like old times, he thought as a smirk tipped up one corner of his mouth.

He'd seen her in recent years, even chatted with her when he'd worked security for her sister,

Liz, and her then-boyfriend, Ian, but Heath hadn't been alone with Maddie like this since high school.

He cranked the engine and turned up the heat to ward off the chill of the late February night before fumbling in the truck door for a plastic bag. "If you get sick, puke in this. Having a three-year-old little girl makes it nearly impossible to keep my truck clean, so every little bit helps."

"I'll try to not hurl in your truck, even though I have a bad track record. You're bringing me home drunk again, just like the good old days." A loud and unladylike belch popped out of her pretty mouth. She giggled. "Sorry. I guess that's nothing to brag about, huh? Gosh, if my kids saw me like this… I'm still scarred from seeing Mama drunk when I was young."

"Don't worry, sweetheart. I'm sure they're sound asleep at this hour." He winked. "I hope your dad is, too. And *not* waiting with a shotgun."

"He wasn't gonna shoot you though, Heath-bar. He knew you'd take care of me. Hopefully, Mama won't be up to put my drunk ass in the shower with all my clothes on." She snorted. "I can't remember that guy's name we were riding around with, but I won't forget putting away a fifth of Thunderbird." She shuddered.

He grinned. "She was trying to sober you up." The idea of taking her to the lake at Southland and tossing her in filled him with a sense of mischief, reminding him of all the times they swam there growing up.

He glanced over, and in the dim light, her face crumpled. *Great. A blubbering drunk woman.*

"Mad, what's wrong?"

"Heath," she sucked in a shaky breath, "in case I forgot to tell you, I've always loved you. You were one of my best friends, and I'm sorry I didn't stay in touch." Her words slurred, and tears streamed down her cheeks.

Pressing his lips together to suppress a smile, he waited a beat before he spoke. "I know. I've always loved you too, and you know I'd do anything in the world for you and your family." He wrinkled his nose. "Except hide the dead bodies."

She laughed and snapped her fingers. "Darn." Her expression turned serious again, but the tears ceased. "I'm real proud of you for taking your niece and raising her. Not many single men would've wanted the responsibility, but you're a good man." She patted his arm and held on with a squeeze.

His heart warmed, the same as his skin under her touch. He'd secretly harbored a crush on Maddie Baker since elementary school. She'd been back home with her folks at Southland for several months, but he'd purposely avoided her for fear his old feelings would resurface.

When Maddie's dad, Big Dan, had his heart attack two summers before, Heath had tried to bypass Maddie then, too. Seeing her with her husband tortured Heath. He had never liked the man, and now he hated him for hurting her. Heath would never understand how his Maddie wound up as a prissy, city doctor's wife. Not that she wasn't good enough. It just didn't fit. She was sunshine, blue skies, tall pines, boots, leather, and horse's hair. Shoot, just about anything with four legs and fur loved her. Heath had always insisted she should be a vet, but Maddie had wanted to contribute to the family business by becoming a nurse. From a distance, Heath could see she'd buried part of herself. The parts he loved most. Still loved. The parts he hoped she'd reclaim by coming home.

A soft snore escaped Maddie when he turned off the dirt road from the bar and onto the blacktop. Her hand still rested on his arm, so he shifted, twining his fingers with hers.

They'd been close friends all through school and had gotten in trouble together many times, but he could never tell her how much he truly cared for her. He valued her friendship so much the risk of losing her, if she didn't return his feelings, crippled him. Like she'd told Ricky earlier, Heath was like a brother. She had enough brothers. Heath had wanted to be more, but he'd lost her anyway.

Turning in the drive at Southland, he stopped to enter the code, which opened the gate. It hadn't changed since he'd last worked for the family.

At the sound of the metal gears, Maddie startled awake, looked around, and then dozed off again with a little smile on her lips.

The estate covered several hundred acres and boasted a large main house with three standalone cottages. As far as Heath knew, the caretakers still lived in one cabin, and one of Maddie's brothers was in another. Other buildings on the property included a six-car garage, a barn, and a woodshed. The latter was where the kids were taken when they needed discipline. Heath was glad he'd never visited that little stone structure.

He pulled up to the main house and stopped.

Johnny, Maddie's brother, sat on the back porch, smoking a cigarette. Heath cut the engine and got out as Johnny approached.

"Hey, Cookie Monster." Johnny called him by the nickname he'd given Heath in high school as they shook hands. "What's up?"

"I brought Maddie home. She's pretty well trashed. Where should I take her?"

"Tied one on, did she? Well, she deserves it after that sumbitch broke her heart." He thumped his cigarette, and it flew several feet to land on the packed dirt lane. "Take her down to the last cottage; the door's unlocked. That'll keep her kids from waking her up at the ass-crack of dawn. I've trained my boy to sleep in."

Heath let out a short bark of laughter. "How's Nick doing?"

"Keeps me busy. He loves having his cousins out here when he visits on weekends. They play hard and wear each other out. How's that cute little one of yours?"

"She's a handful. I'm up to my eyeballs in pink tutus and Hello Kitty." Heath ran a hand through his hair.

"It's a good thing God gave me a boy." Johnny patted Heath's back. "More power to you, brother."

Heath said goodnight and drove down the lane, deeper into the property. It'd been a long time since he'd been out there. Even in the dark, it was a beautiful place, full of magic and memories.

At the cottage, he carried Maddie inside and laid her on the bed. He sat next to her and brushed a strand of auburn hair from her face, fantasizing about many things. Her mothering his daughter was one of them. Since Willow Creek was a small town and people knew his family, many still called her his niece, but he'd adopted her, and she'd become his little girl. His baby needed a good mother. One like the woman he'd loved most of his life.

He sighed. Maddie had been through so much in the recent past. He couldn't burden her by baring his heart. On the other hand, his daughter wasn't a burden; she was irresistible. All he'd have to do would be to introduce them and see what happened.

Snapping out of his delusion, he wavered. Maddie was too fragile, and she had her own kids to worry about.

"He was a fool to let you go, Maddie-cake." He kissed her forehead and left her sleeping.

Chapter Two

The remnants of a dream clung to Maddie. She was riding Leroy hard and fast. He barely slowed as they made the turn to follow the creek.

The wind in her face helped clear her head and heart from the trauma of the previous summer when her perfect little world fell apart. It had been one of those days when she thought, *Life is good.* But life had slapped her up 'side the head and laughed as she'd writhed on the floor in agony.

Not wanting to relive her heartache in her sleep, Maddie sat up, forcing herself awake. A moment later, she lay back down, *literally* writhing in agony.

Gripping her head to keep her alcohol soaked brain from exploding, she took a deep breath. The wave of nausea passed, and she opened her eyes again.

It took her a moment to get her bearings. Her initial thought was, *Oh hell, I must've spent the night with Ricky.* When she recognized her surroundings as the guest cottage, she let out an audible sigh.

"I'm never drinking again." She pressed her palm against her forehead to stave off the pounding.

About that time, her kids and her nephew came through the front door.

"Mama."

"Aunt Maddie, get up."

The volume of the throbs in her head increased at their shouts. "Shh, kiddos. I got me a headache."

"Daddy said you're probably hung over," Nick, her six-year-old nephew, offered.

"What's hung over?" Josh, her six-year-old son, asked.

"Remember what I told you about repeating things Uncle Johnny says. He can get you in trouble," Maddie told her youngest as she sat up and pulled him in for a hug.

"It's true," Nick said. "I get in trouble with my mom all the time when I repeat things Daddy says."

Johnny came in followed by Heath, who carried his daughter. More adorable than Maddie could have imagined and with a dimple to match Heath's, the little girl peeked out from behind thick, dark lashes. Seeing him in his role as a daddy made something tighten deep within Maddie. A strange sense of nostalgia and a lost hope welled up.

It had been Maddie's fear that Heath would make the rodeo his home and never settle down. All the sad country songs about the cowboy riding away still made Maddie change the station. Remembering Heath and the friendship they'd once shared had bothered her since the day he loaded his new quarter horse on a rickety, old trailer and drove south.

Jenny, her eight-year-old, tugged Maddie's hand, causing her to snap out of the past. There was nothing that could change it anyway, and seeing him settled in Willow Creek gave Maddie a new happiness to hold onto.

"We've got company, Mama," Jenny said. "Mr. Heath brought Sara Ann to see our horses. She's kinda scared of theirs."

The little girl buried her face in Heath's neck, and Maddie daydreamed about doing the same. The smell of his aftershave wafted through the air and tickled Maddie's nose. Her olfactory senses weren't the only ones awakened at the scent or the sight of him.

"She's shy at first, but she usually warms up." Heath tweaked her nose. "Isn't that right, sweet pea?"

She shook her head no, and the kids laughed.

"Come on, Mama. Let's go show Sara Ann the horses." Jenny would've pulled Maddie slap out of the bed if Maddie hadn't been worried about being undressed.

"All right, I'm up already." Maddie lifted the cover and glanced down at last night's clothes. "I need to go up to the house to change real quick. I'll meet y'all at the barn."

Maddie gave Sara Ann a little finger wave after Heath turned to go. A bashful smile greeted Maddie just before the little pink lips burrowed against her daddy's shoulder—a big, muscled shoulder that bulged beneath his plaid button down.

Damn, Mad. Stop lusting after the man. Friend, remember? But why did he have to be so damn hot?

***

Heath tried not to stare when Maddie strode up to the corral. In cowboy boots, nicely fitted jeans, and a T-shirt, which hugged every curve of her upper body, he had to force his mouth shut.

When did she get those?

She'd always been beautiful, but thirty-two had never looked better on a woman.

Maddie climbed up, threw her leg over the rail, and sat on the top of the fence next to him. She tied her hair up in a messy knot. "I thought any kid of yours would be on the circuit by now, Heath-bar."

"She rides with me, but she's not real sure about riding on her own just yet." To his daughter he said, "Did you know Miss Maddie was a barrel racing champion and trick rider when we were kids?"

An exaggerated shake of her head signaled she didn't.

"Did you know that your daddy and I were team roping champions?" Maddie asked the little girl. "Your daddy's still the best roper I've ever seen."

Sara Ann's smile made her eyes sparkle. "Daddy ropes me sometimes."

Maddie winked. "I bet he does. Let's see if we've still got it."

Maddie hopped off the fence and disappeared into the barn. She returned with rope. When the older kids saw it, they left the horses they were petting and came running.

"We want to try," they said.

Maddie, Johnny, and Heath knotted ropes for everyone, and they practiced roping the fence posts. Before long, the kids were trying to rope each other.

A grateful smile flitted across Heath's face because Sara Ann allowed Jenny to take her under her wing and show her how to work the lariat. Worry always niggled the back of his mind that his girl was missing out by not having a female presence in her life.

"Jenny thinks she has a baby doll to play with." Maddie nodded to their girls. "She *is* a doll baby; that's for sure."

"Well, I can't take credit for that," he said.

"I know you hate hearing this because it still bothers me a little when people mistake me for Liz, but you and your brother looked a lot alike. Sara Ann could pass for yours," Maddie said, a smile raised the rosy pads of her cheeks. "I always had a crush on your brother. He was good lookin'."

"You did?" One of Heath's eyebrows crawled higher.

"Yes, don't you remember? I used to act like a complete idiot around him. If he looked my way or heaven forbid, spoke to me, I'd giggle like an idiot."

"Not to interrupt you two lovebirds," Johnny stepped between them and put a hand on each of their shoulders, "but I'm putting together a team for a charity clay shoot. Y'all interested?"

"I'm in," Heath said, intentionally ignoring the lovebird comment. No need to show his hand or his heart. "How 'bout you Maddie-cake? Can you still shoot, or did getting attacked by a target machine put you off the sport?"

For a split second, she stalled, eyes wide, and then her breath escaped in a rush of laughter. "I still have the scar to remind me. As long as I'm behind the sights of the shotgun and not near the trap thrower, I'm good."

"I thought your mama was gonna kill me when she barreled into the ER that day. Her hair was on fire." Heath had been horrified when Maddie had gotten hurt on his watch.

"None of the trouble I got into was your fault, but you were always there, and that made you an accessory to the crime." She winked and poked him with one slim finger.

Heat flared in his chest, and he grabbed her hand, squeezing it once before he let it go. Reconnecting with Maddie spurred hope, but he couldn't let it take root. Sara Ann was his priority, and he didn't want to introduce someone into her life who might not be around for the long haul.

It had been a mistake to come back to Southland.

Chapter Three

Maddie stifled a groan when Mark's car pulled up. "Jenny, Josh, your dad's here."

In his excitement, Josh forgot about the gate, climbed over the fence, and ran to greet his dad.

Jenny picked Sara Ann up and set her on her hip. "Mama, Dad's got Christy with him again. I can't stand her."

Maddie took Sara Ann from her daughter. "Jenny, remember your manners." She hated saying that. "I know it's difficult, but I think she's trying to get to know you guys. That's a good thing, right?"

"I guess. Can I stay here with you?" Jenny asked, her lip poking out a mile.

"No, baby. Your daddy gets you tonight," Maddie said. "You guys are going to the aquarium, I think. That'll be fun. And then I'll pick you up tomorrow."

Maddie handed Sara Ann off to Heath and walked Jenny over to the car where Mark waited.

Seeing her ex and the home wrecker always made her stomach churn. Forcing the taste of bile down, she fought for a pleasant expression for her kids' sakes. They gave her goodbye kisses and climbed in the backseat. Christy turned around to speak to them.

"Who's the guy?" Mark stood inside his open car door, his yellow golf shirt picking up the lighter flecks in his shit brown eyes. His close-cropped hair showed very little of the natural blond highlights Maddie had once loved.

She glanced back toward the corral. Part of her wanted to play up having a hot, single man visiting. But the other part didn't want any more drama. "Oh, that's Heath. He's a friend of ours. Remember, he helped with security for Lizabelle and Ian when Big Daddy was in the hospital?"

"The State Trooper?" Mark asked.

She nodded and kicked at a small rock.

"Wait a second. Is he the same guy you used to run around with in high school?" Mark closed the car door and stepped toward her.

"What does it matter, Mark? You're here to pick up our kids with your girlfriend, the one you got while still married to me. Who I run around with past, present, or future is none of your business."

His chest expanded with breath. "As long as our kids are involved, it is my business."

"Really?" Maddie's hands landed on her hips. "I wonder what the custody judge would say if she knew the home wrecker living with you worked as a stripper to pay for nursing school?" His shocked expression caused a smug tilt to her lips. "That's right, Mark. I'm not as dumb as I look. Shove that up your tailpipe and don't ever threaten me over my children."

As she watched the cheater and his *lover* drive away with her kids, Maddie's hair was on fire just like Heath had said her mama's had been. The classic temper redheads were famous for graced her and her siblings, but Maddie might've gotten an extra measure of it.

Luck had been on Mark's side the day she'd discovered his infidelity. If she hadn't been so devastated, she would've killed his ass. Or at least maimed him.

Her whole body had shaken from pain and shame and anger. Maddie had done the first thing any southern woman did in a crisis. She'd called her mama.

***

Heath kept an eye on Sara Ann and Nick, who practiced with their ropes, and tried to ignore Maddie dealing with her ex. He knew what those hands on her hips used to mean. She'd take crap up to a certain point, then explode like a volcano. It would be fun to see her tear that guy a new asshole. But maybe not with her kids watching.

Maddie strolled over and leaned against the fence between him and Johnny. "I think cheaters should get mandatory castration."

"Whoa, sister," Johnny said. "That reeks of bitterness."

"Damn right, I'm bitter." She lowered her eyes.

Heath could feel the shame radiating from her,

and he wanted to kick some ass. With Johnny there, Heath kept the comfort he longed to offer to himself. She was obviously still hung up on Dr. Mark. He couldn't risk getting close and revealing his feelings, not when he had Sara Ann to protect.

"Do you think she'll ride with me?" Maddie's voice interrupted his thoughts.

Blinking, he tore his gaze away from his daughter and shrugged. "Probably not, but we can ask."

To his surprise, Sara Ann said yes and seemed excited about the prospect. They saddled up horses for everyone and rode around the corral.

Heath laughed as Sara Ann tried tossing the catch rope from the saddle. It took a few tries, but she finally got the fencepost with Maddie's help. Heath's chest swelled with pride for his little girl and with something else for Maddie. He needed to guard himself better.

"We're going to get Daisy to trot around the corral now, Sara Ann. Let me know if we go too fast, okay?"

Heath waited, expecting Sara Ann to kick up a fuss. But the squeal she let out was one of delight, and his smile widened.

"This is fun," Sara Ann said with a breathy laugh.

"It sure is, sweet girl," Maddie said. "How would you like to ride down to see the lake?"

"Can Daddy come, too?" she asked, eyebrows lifted.

"Of course, I'm coming. I can't let you leave me in the dust, sweet pea." He kissed two of his fingers and then reached over to pat her hand, which rested on the pommel.

Maddie caught his hand as it retreated and gave it a quick squeeze. His chest mimicked her movement.

Johnny and Nick rode in front, with Heath and Maddie trailing them. Heath struggled not to stare at his old friend.

"Thanks for this. She's really having a good time," Heath said.

"So am I." Maddie hugged his baby with one arm.

"Go faster," Sara Ann said. "Catch Nick."

"Okay, cutie. Hold on." Maddie nudged Daisy to a fast trot.

Heath laughed at Sara Ann's squawk of laughter as he clicked his tongue and galloped to catch up.

The woods at Southland were like a second home to him. As they entered the clearing around the lake, memories flooded his mind. He and Maddie, always together. Always laughing. To say he'd missed it was an understatement. More than the surroundings, he missed the girl. His best friend. He stayed lost in thought all the way back to the barn.

After their ride, it was nap time for Sara Ann. Maddie walked them to the truck and hugged Sara Ann tight, kissing her forehead before passing her to Heath, so he could put her in her car seat.

"I never thanked you for rescuing me and bringing me home last night. I hope I didn't say anything to embarrass myself." Her gaze darted to the ground before it returned to his.

"Hey, it's me you're talking to. I know almost every embarrassing thing about you, at least from back in the day." He started to get in the truck, but turned around to her again. "I won't tell anyone you tried to kiss me last night."

"Ugh, I did not." She swatted his arm. "Did I?"

He grinned, enjoying the way she squirmed. "No." *But I wish you had.*

Stepping away, she stuck her hands in her pockets. "Today was fun. Come back anytime. Y'all have a standing invitation."

"Thanks, I'll see you later." He intended to give her a quick peck, but while aiming for her cheek, his lips landed awfully close to hers. He lingered to inhale her earthy scent. When her breath hitched and her chest lifted, bumping into him, he turned to go.

By sheer will power, he didn't let himself look in the rearview mirror. After he pulled his truck onto the road, he took a deep breath and glanced back to see Sara Ann, her eyelids heavy.

The joy his little girl gave him lifted his soul to a new high. Keeping her safe and happy was his job, and he considered it his honor.

***

When the dust settled, Maddie headed back toward the house.

Damn, Heath smelled good. I better stay sober around him from now on or else I really might try to kiss him.

She touched the spot on her face, which still tingled from where his lips had landed.

21

Johnny met her on the back porch steps. "I never understood why you two didn't get together, Mad."

"We're just friends, bro. I know it's a foreign concept to you, to have a female friend, but that's what we are."

"I don't know." He tilted his head to one side. "I always thought he kinda had the hots for you."

"Did not. Shut it, Johnny." She slugged him in the arm.

Johnny pretended it hurt even as he held the back door open for her.

Mama D met them at the door. "Was that Heath and Sara Ann? Isn't she just precious? Why didn't they come in?"

"Yes, ma'am, that was them. It's nap time. For me, too." Maddie started for the stairs.

"I always told you Heath was a keeper. You should've dated him."

Maddie turned on her heel. "Mama, I'm pretty sure that you telling me I should date him made me not want to. You know how teenagers are or at least, how I was. Whatever you and Big Daddy said I should do, I wanted to do the opposite. In fact, I did do the opposite most of the time."

"Oh, child. I thought the boys were hard to handle as teens, but then you came along and put them all to shame. You were my rebel." Her mama half smiled.

"And proud of it." Maddie nodded once. "Let's just pray my kids don't act out like I did."

"Sister, don't you remember when we used to get in trouble, and Mama D would say, '*One day, I hope you have ten kids just like you?*'" Johnny asked.

"Lord, yes, I remember. That would be payback of the worst kind."

"Uh-huh," Mama D said. "What goes around comes around, don't cha know?"

Maddie and Johnny looked at each other. "We're in trouble," they said in unison.

Maddie crawled under the covers and thought about *the keeper*. Heath's dimple could stop a girl's heart. She'd always loved that particular facial feature, always wanted to touch it. His brother had had one just like it. But Heath liked her as a friend.

He'd gone through plenty of girlfriends back then, all of whom hated Maddie out of pure jealousy. His black hair and ice blue eyes were hard to resist. Oh, and the muscles. He was a gym rat, even in high school. Now, his biceps must measure twenty inches or more. But Maddie had always been in the friend zone. That was okay. She'd rather be his friend, someone who meant something to him, instead of another notch in his belt.

When she'd told him she had a crush on his brother, it was true. But she had a crush on Heath, too. *Still*.

She sighed. There wasn't anything she could do about it now. And since she was a bitter divorcee with two kids, it wasn't likely she'd ever find love again.

Chapter Four

The next time Maddie saw Heath was at the charity clay shoot. She'd thought of him every day, but each time she almost called, she talked herself out of it.

He has his own life. He doesn't want to hang out with someone who wasn't woman enough to hold onto her husband.

"Hey, Heath-bar," she said when he approached, carrying his shotgun and a box of shells.

"Maddie-cake, Johnny, Big Dan." He shook hands with her dad and brother and gave her a side hug.

Definitely in the friend zone.

"How's the cutie-pie?" Maddie asked.

"I'm fine, thanks for asking." He smiled, showing off that damn dimple.

"I meant your baby girl, but you're a cutie-pie too." She pinched his arm playfully, but then she held on and squeezed his biceps. "Damn, Heath. It's time to get off the juice. No wonder you aren't married yet." She lowered her voice. "That stuff can make it so you can't perform. You know…please your woman."

He raised his eyebrows. "My baby girl is fine. She's with my dad this morning." He dipped his chin so his mouth was close to her ear. "You know good and damn well I'm not on any *juice* and my performance is just fine."

"Ooh, prove it."

Why did I say that? Don't be an idiot, Maddie. Don't lose a lifelong friend over a stupid joke.

"I'm just teasing you." Her face radiated heat like the surface of the sun.

"I'll show you how well I can perform…shooting sporting clays. Will that do?" His voice was teasing, and his mouth begged to be kissed.

"Ab-absolutely." The funny thing was the look he'd given her, when she'd told him to prove it, made the *old girl* feel alive for the first time since she'd discovered her husband was sticking it to his nurse.

Maybe you're still in working order, even if we have to knock the dust off.

A one-night rodeo with Heath would set her up for a while. She gave him a seductive smile, one she'd never aimed at him on purpose. Then she gave herself a mental bitch-slap.

Don't run off your only friend.

Maddie turned her attention to the reason they were together.

When her team won the charity shoot, guilt scampered at the edges of Maddie's mind. The Bakers had their own private firing range at Southland. She and her siblings had been shooting since childhood, and Maddie had gotten plenty of practice since her first and last date with Ricky "All Hands" Dalton.

"Congratulations, sugar." Big Daddy nodded toward her Annie Oakley Award trophy as he slid his arm around her shoulders.

"Thanks, Daddy," she replied, as they made their way to the trucks.

"I'll buy the beer to celebrate," Johnny said.

"I have to go get my girl," Heath said.

"Bring your daddy and baby, and y'all come out to Southland for supper," Big Daddy said.

"Thank you. I think my dad has a dinner date tonight, but Sara Ann and I are free. What can we bring?"

The thrill coursing through Maddie needed to be tamped down, but she'd missed Heath, and any opportunity to spend time with him brightened her day. If she could stop ogling his butt in those Wranglers, she might make it through the night.

***

Big Dan told Heath not to bring anything but himself and his pretty little girl, but Heath wasn't about to show up empty handed. He let Sara Ann carry the flowers for the ladies of the house. He carried juice boxes in one hand and a case of beer in the other.

His daughter danced up to the front steps, wearing leggings under a pink tutu and carrying the bouquet that was almost as big as she was. He hadn't expected the responsibility of raising his deceased brother and sister-in-law's baby, but he wouldn't give her up for the world.

In his mind, being a good father also meant teaching her how a real man should treat a lady. They had date nights, and he always got her flowers. He wanted her to know the difference between a good man and one who was unworthy of her time and attention. It wouldn't be a problem for years to come, but she needed to be ready. She was *his* to teach and protect, and he meant to do it right.

Maddie opened the door to greet them and dropped to her knees. "Well, hello, gorgeous," she said to Sara Ann. "You, too." Her eyes flitted to his, and she winked.

His heart flipped in his chest, and blood flow increased to a certain organ situated below his belt. He shifted his weight from foot to foot.

"Did your daddy give you flowers?" Maddie asked.

"Sometimes he gives me flowers, but we brought these for you, right Daddy?" Sara Ann looked up at him.

He cleared his throat. "They are for Miss Maddie *and* Miss Dixie."

"Thank you. They're beautiful." Maddie took the bouquet. "Can I have a hug?"

By the time she got her hug, her kids were crowding around the door.

"Come on, Sara Ann. Let's go play." Jenny took his baby's hand and they were off.

Heath held out his other offerings as Maddie

got to her feet.

"Beer and juice boxes. Good combination." She laughed and took the juice boxes. "Come on in." She led him to the kitchen.

"Umph-umph-ummm. Well, look at you, young man, all grown up and handsome as pie." The elderly housekeeper wiped her hands on her apron.

"Hello, Miss May. You're looking very well." Heath kissed the cheek of the woman who'd been at Southland as long as he could remember.

She hugged his neck. "It sho' is good to see you, Heath Cook. You're a good apple. I always told Maddie, didn't I?"

"Yes, ma'am. Good as an apple and sweet as a peach. That's my Heath." Maddie grinned, seemingly happy about the attention aimed at him.

Maddie's mama, Dixie, hugged him and thanked him for the flowers before ushering him into the living room where the guys were watching Atlanta Braves baseball on the big screen.

Maddie came in and handed him a beer. "You okay with Sara Ann playing upstairs with the kids?"

"Of course. She loves Jenny and Josh and Nick. I'll check on her in a little while. Come sit with me." Heath patted the couch next to him.

Maddie squeezed in between him and Johnny and sipped her beer.

"I wasn't sure you'd ever drink again after I found you at Mason's the other night," he said.

"Moderation is the key." She nodded and clinked her beer bottle against his. "Isn't Sara Ann in Pre-K? Do you guys have plans for Spring

Break?"

"Yes and no. I took the week off, so I can take her somewhere, but sadly, I haven't planned where we're going. I thought about a big amusement park, but I think she's a little young."

"Oh. My. God." Johnny sat forward on the couch. "I have just the thing. I forgot to tell you, Mad, but when I picked Nick up yesterday, Tiffany told me she wants to take him skiing for Spring Break. Her parents rented a place in Colorado."

"So…that means we have two tickets for a kid-friendly cruise up for grabs," Maddie said, raising her eyebrows at Heath.

"Are you serious?" Heath asked.

"Yeah. Johnny and Nick's suite is adjoining mine and my kids. It's yours if you want it," she said.

"Well…" Flustered didn't begin to describe his reaction. He didn't know what to say. "Ah…I don't know. Send me the dates of everything, and I'll check to be sure we can do it. And please, for the love of all that's holy, don't mention it to Sara Ann yet. She'll go nuts." An embarrassing thought hit him in his right butt cheek where his wallet was nestled. "Let me know the cost, so I can pay you for the tickets."

"Uh-uh." Johnny held a hand up. "My treat if you can make it. Otherwise, it's just lost."

"No way." Heath's face warmed. "I'll just give you the money I would've spent at Disney World."

"Check your calendar. We'll discuss it when the time comes." Johnny leaned back.

Heath hoped he could work it out, but he also

hoped it wouldn't break the bank. The little life insurance his brother Glenn had had was in an account earmarked for Sara Ann's college fund.

The Bakers didn't have to worry about money, so they did things big. The prospect of vacationing with his daughter and his favorite female and her kids was a good one. But he and his girl weren't a charity case, and he refused to go if he couldn't pay their way.

Chapter Five

The cruise ship practically vibrated with the energy of the crew and kids as families boarded. Maddie couldn't contain her smile as Jenny and Josh bounced, screeching in delight. When they took off to see the costumed characters, Sara Ann kicked her feet until Heath put her down. For a moment, she hesitated, clinging to the cargo pocket on her daddy's shorts, but then she skipped and hopped through the crowd until she hugged the leg of someone dressed like a horse.

"A girl after my own heart," Maddie said, almost to herself.

The crease of Heath's brow contradicted the upturned corners of his lips. Maddie had had the same fear and awe on their first cruise, but Mark had been by her side. At one time, she'd thought she could do anything with his support. Slowly, she was learning her own strength.

Spring Break the previous year had been their

last vacation together as a family, and it had ended early for Maddie when Liz had her baby prematurely. It was not, however, Maddie's last adventure with Mark. That had been their ill-fated ten year anniversary getaway to the Florida Keys. Not even a hurricane could wipe out the memory of his betrayal, which she'd discovered on the last day of their trip.

Pressure built behind her eyes and tightened her chest as the old hurt slammed into her. Turning her head away from Heath, she tamped down the welling emotion. Mark wasn't worth her tears. Sure, they'd had ten good years and two beautiful kids together, but he'd made the choice to break up their family, not her. She refused to let him take up residence in her mind anymore. Her marriage was over, and she needed a fresh start.

"You okay?" Heath nudged her arm.

Surprised, Maddie turned quickly and elbowed Heath, catching him in the ribs. She immediately pressed her hand over the area to soothe it. A wall of muscle greeted her. "Sorry 'bout that. I'm fine, and I'm glad you guys came with us."

"You still have bony elbows. Those things are weapons." He cupped the offending body part with his palm, even as a big smile broke out across his face. "I'm glad we came, too."

That darn dimple would be her undoing. Or maybe it would be the hard muscles. From hurt to lust in a split second. Maddie needed to get control of herself before she jumped on her best friend and rode him like a bucking bronco.

Her cheeks flamed, and she prayed he couldn't

read her mind.

The kids returned, a welcomed distraction, and Maddie put her arms around them. "Are y'all ready to party?"

***

Heath's senses hit high alert with all the activity on board the ship. He'd never seen so many little people together in one place. The sheer size of the ship intimidated him, and he was a grown man. On the other hand, Sara Ann looked like she'd found heaven on earth. Thankfully, this wasn't Maddie's first rodeo, and her calm presence reassured him. The last thing he wanted was to appear weak in her eyes, so he forced the deer-in-the-headlights expression from his face.

He closed the cabin door and leaned against it. A strange deafness occurred from the lack of noise. It only took a few moments before Josh and Jenny pounded on the door adjourning their suites.

Their voices joined with Sara Ann's as they begged to go swimming in the puppy dog pool.

Maddie winked at him from the open doorway. "Let's get our suits."

His imagination ran wild with ideas of the sexy redhead in her birthday suit.

Damn, Heath. Knock it off.

Shaking his head, he opened Sara Ann's suitcase and pink tulle fell out. He chuckled, wishing his brother were there to see it. The little ache of missing Glenn was often overshadowed by the joy of raising his daughter.

The purple bathing suit dangled from his finger, and he held it just high enough so Sara Ann couldn't reach it when she jumped.

"Daddy, give me." Her voice vibrated with a giggle.

"What's the magic word?"

She leaped again, a near miss. "Pleeeaaassseee," she sang. "Pretty please with sugar on top."

He scooped her up and kissed her cheek. "Well, since you asked so nicely."

Jenny darted into the room. "Hurry up, hurry up."

If they were going to be this fired up all week, he was gonna be worn out. In a flash, he had Sara Ann fixed up in sparkly, purple lycra with two rows of ruffles on the butt. Jenny and Josh each took one of her hands, while their little hodge-podge family walked together to one of the many pools onboard. Heath was grateful Maddie's children had taken Sara Ann under their wings.

"You aren't going to believe this right now," Maddie said, "but by the end of the trip, you'll be much more relaxed. This cruise line does this thing right. The kids have a blast and so do the grown-ups." She wriggled her eyebrows.

They angled lounge chairs, so they could keep an eye on their brood. Heath lost focus when Maddie took off her cover-up to reveal a dark turquoise bikini, which matched the color of her eyes. She'd always had a nice body and having two kids hadn't changed that. The main difference was in her top.

"What? Too much?" She scrunched her nose. "They're bigger than I originally intended, but now that I'm used to them, I think they're all right."

He gaped. *Better than all right. Dayum.* "You won't hear me complaining, but you were what? An A before? Now, what? D?"

"Good eye, my friend. You always did know your boobs."

"What's that supposed to mean?" He paused as he was about to pull his T-shirt over his head.

"Oh, come on. You never dated a small-chested girl back in the day. Your women were stacked. I was always so jealous." She adjusted the back on her chair.

"So you thought getting bigger ones would get you noticed?" He furrowed his brow. "By whom?"

Her cheeks grew pink as the muscle in her jaw twitched, and she glanced away before she spoke. "Don't all men prefer bigger ones to smaller ones?"

"I can't speak for all men. Like I said, you won't hear any complaints from me one way or the other. You were beautiful before." He let his words hang in the air. "And you're beautiful now. But I'd say your money was well spent."

A near audible sigh escaped her. "Thank you, Heath. It's nice to know you approve." She wiggled in her seat. "Are you planning to sunbathe in your T-shirt? Or are you gonna take it off and make all the females drool?"

He shook his head before he slipped the thin cotton over his head.

"Nice." Her tongue darted out as she licked her lips. "I have a hot bod to stare at during my vacay."

"So do I." He leaned back in his chair and smiled at her.

***

By dinnertime each night, the kids were worn out from going hard all day long. Maddie had fallen hard for Sara Ann and loved how the little sweetie wanted Maddie to help tuck her in at night. The children wanted to sleep in the same bed, so Maddie and Heath got to tuck them all in together. The domesticity felt natural, but Maddie wouldn't let her mind follow that train of thought. It lead to unfulfilled expectations.

"Miss Maddie, do you know who's my favorite princess?" Sara Ann asked her one night.

"No, baby. Who is it?"

"You." Sara Ann played with Maddie's hair. "I like your hair, and you sing real pretty. My daddy could be your prince."

Maddie didn't look at Heath, fearing a setup. But in her heart she knew young children got their own ideas, and it was easy to see why Sara Ann would wish for a fairytale. They'd inadvertently given her reason to hope.

"Your daddy is one of my most favorite princes ever, and you're one of the prettiest princesses I've ever seen." Maddie planted a kiss on her forehead.

She giggled and then quieted, so Maddie could sing the goodnight song. After they gave each child a kiss, she and Heath retired to the other suite for a nightcap. They propped their feet up and sipped beer, complaining about being old. Their parents would spank them if they overheard. Watching the kids have fun was nearly as tiring as participating in the fun themselves.

As they laughed together over their new

memories, Maddie was reminded of how much she enjoyed Heath's company. She could almost look at him without wanting to caress his rock hard abs. *Almost*.

Later that night, alone in her room, Maddie reached for the zipper on the back of her dress. After an unsuccessful struggle, she remembered Jenny had helped her with it earlier. She bit her lip as she debated on bothering Heath, but she had little choice.

Trying to be quiet, she tapped on Heath's bathroom door. It opened, revealing the body of a god in boxers. *Damn boxers*.

Saliva pooled at the corners of her mouth. Wicked fantasies sprang to life as she continued to stare at his bare chest.

For goodness sake, they were in the Caribbean and spent every day by the pool or on a beach. He should've been an old hat by now, but she doubted she'd ever get tired of that view.

"Can you unzip me?" She turned her back to him and lifted her hair.

As his fingers worked the zipper, they grazed her skin, making her tingle all over as chills raced along her spine. Her mind galloped to the place she'd been trying to keep it away from. The place where she acted on her body's urges to throw a bridle on Heath and have her way with him. She was a horse's hair away from taking action, so she stepped away when the zipper was low enough.

"Thanks, Heath-bar. Sweet dreams." When she looked back and saw him watching her, flag flying at half-mast, she smiled to herself.

***

Heath's feet itched to follow Maddie back to her room and help her out of her dress…and whatever she wore beneath it. The attraction between them grew stronger every day, and being in close quarters with her fanned the flame of desire. If they weren't careful, the fire alarms might go off. It was a fun image, until the thought of waking the children squashed his libido.

Jenny and Josh had him wrapped around their fingers. They missed having a father figure around, and Josh, especially, had latched onto Heath, always hanging on his every word. It was sweet, but the weight of the responsibility tensed the muscles in his neck. If he said the wrong thing and it got back to Mark, Maddie would hear about it. Only nails rivaled her in toughness, and she could handle herself, but he didn't want to be culpable for any more crap raining down on her from Mark.

Early on, Heath often caught her lost in thought—probably reminiscing about her last cruise when she was still married to Mark. If there was someone Heath wanted to punch in the throat, it was that guy for hurting Maddie. In an attempt to help her and satisfy his own curiosity, one night Heath had asked her what had happened.

"We were getting ready to go home after celebrating ten years of wedded bliss." She glanced at him and then returned her gaze to the water. "More like wedded blindness on my part. Mark was in the shower, and his cell phone buzzed. Since he's a doctor, I thought I'd be the good wife and check it for him. That text message knocked me on my ass."

Her eyes were unfocused.

"'*Can't wait to see you tonight, lover.*' That's what the text from Christy said. First of all, who the hell was Christy and why was she texting Mark on *our* anniversary trip and making plans to see him that night? And who calls somebody lover? Must've been a wrong number, I thought. Stupid me." She shook her head.

Heath took her hand and offered a comforting squeeze.

"I scrolled back through the messages and found it was the right number. The night before, after we had…you know…sex, while I slept, *my* husband sent a text to that woman. I'll never forget it. '*I can't wait to hold you in my arms again.*'" Her voice dripped with disgust. "He never said shit like that to me. Bastard."

They were on the balcony of her suite, and their kids slept inside. Heath dragged her chair closer and put his arms around her. "Honey, I'm so sorry."

She leaned against his chest and wiped her eyes. "No. I'm sorry. I don't mean to get so emotional. It just hurts, ya know?"

Heath didn't know. He'd never let himself get that close to anyone, but his heart hurt for her. And for the loss of the once stable life she'd built with Mark.

"How soon before you moved back to Southland?" he asked, sliding his hand up and down her arm.

"Within a few days. It was almost time for school to start, and I didn't want the kids moving a week into it. Willow Creek's got good schools. I mean, we turned out all right, didn't we?" She tilted her face up toward him.

A chuckle rumbled in his chest. "Damn right, we did."

"They didn't really like that uppity private school anyway. My kids are country, like me."

It was true. Everything about country living suited Maddie. And coming home got Maddie back to one of her first loves—the horses. Southland had been Heath's second home for many years, when he and Maddie were as thick as the pine forest on the property. Memories of their rodeo days always made Heath feel like he belonged. He'd had a place there with her.

"Mark tried to get around the prenup. Claimed that ten years entitled him to more of my trust fund."

"I bet Aunt Nancy straightened him out." Heath had always gotten along very well with Aunt Nancy, who was also the family attorney.

If he remembered right, Maddie had only gotten access to her trust fund two years earlier, when she'd turned thirty. He couldn't even imagine the millions of dollars she had, but that was the thing about her—her and all the Bakers. No one who met them on the street would ever know they were loaded.

"Yep." Maddie wore a shit-eating grin when she looked up at him.

"Nancy's got a black belt in kick-ass-and-take-names." Heath winked.

"Sure does." Maddie's laugh shook her

shoulders. "The judge said a specialty surgeon had enough income to support himself without getting a payout from his wealthy wife's trust. And because we're both financially sound, no one has to pay child support. It helped that I worked our entire marriage, even if it was part-time when the kids were younger."

"Do you miss being a visiting nurse? Or do you like the management stuff?" he asked.

"I miss the people I took care of. There were some crazy times and folks, but supplying home health equipment and care is rewarding. I also like working at the office. I get to see Daddy and Johnny and Paul. Mama comes in sometimes, but she's pretty much turned her stuff over to me. I feel like I'm part of something important."

"You are." He squeezed her and kissed the top of her head.

Later that night, as Heath tried to sleep, an unsettling idea nagged him. The news about Mark wanting Maddie's money hadn't surprised him for some reason. Part of Heath wondered if Dr. Mark had married Maddie, so he could retire early. Heath hated himself for thinking it. How could the man not have been madly in love with the best woman in the world? But in his years as a State Trooper, Heath had seen the worst of humanity. He hoped Mark was just an asshole and not truly a bad guy, but questions remained. Was Mark done trying for Maddie's wealth? If not, how far would he go to get his hands on it?

Chapter Six

Maddie's stomach growled as she got ready for breakfast the next morning, even though she still felt full from dinner the night before. Overeating was par for the course on a cruise ship.

Josh came in from Heath's room, bouncing on the balls of his feet. "Can I go work out with Mr. Heath, Mama? He said it's okay."

She needed to exercise, too. Burn off the nightly visits to the ice cream smorgasbord, but it was vacation. Who exercised on vacation? Heath had to be the only one. As long as she got to keep seeing him shirtless though, she wouldn't complain.

"Work out? Let me see those muscles." Josh flexed his biceps, and she squeezed them. "I don't know, my man. If those guns get any bigger, we'll have to get you some new shirts."

"Mama." He dragged out the two syllable word, making it three.

"Let me check with Mr. Heath to be sure."

"It's fine, Mad," Heath called from the other room. "We need some guy time. Don't we, Josh?"

With wide eyes, Josh nodded his head vigorously.

Too stinking cute. Maddie had fallen in love with him the moment she'd known she was pregnant. She pulled him close and kissed his head five times while he squirmed.

"In that case, the girls and I are going to have breakfast and get mani/pedis. So long, suckers." Maddie winked at Josh, pushing him gently to an arm's length.

"We'll meet you guys for lunch, Maddie-cake." Heath kissed her cheek before he picked Sara Ann up for a hug and kiss. "Be a good girl for Miss Maddie, 'k baby?"

"Okay, Daddy."

Heath and Josh left in their workout clothes— shorts, T-shirts, and sneakers. But the sleeveless T-shirt Heath sported left her wanting to squeeze his guns, too. *Get it together, Mad.*

Having their nails painted turned out to be a huge hit with Sara Ann, whose feet were just as ticklish as Maddie remembered Heath's had been when they were young. She'd made the discovery one of the many nights they'd stayed up late at Southland watching scary movies.

At lunch, the girls showed off their petal pink polish. Josh couldn't have cared less, but Heath melted Maddie's insides when he lavished praise on the impressionable young girls.

Josh cleared his throat. "Mama, I have an important question to ask you."

Maddie placed her hand on his. "What is it, sweet child o' mine?"

"Will you go on a date with me tonight?"

"A real date?" Maddie widened her eyes.

"Yes, ma'am." He nodded.

"I would be honored to go on a date with you, Joshua. What time shall I be ready?"

He looked to Heath who held up seven fingers. "Seven."

Heath spoke up. "I'd like to take Jenny and Sara Ann on a date, too. If they'll allow it."

"Yay!" Sara Ann pumped her arms in the air.

"What about you, Jenny?" Heath asked.

"Is it okay, Mama? Can I go on a date with Mr. Heath and Sara Ann?"

Maddie tilted her head. "I would if I were you."

"Okay. What time shall we be ready?" Jenny repeated Maddie's words.

"I'll pick you up at seven."

"I'll get the girls ready," Maddie told Heath. "Can I send Josh and his clothes over for you to supervise?"

"Absolutely," Heath said. "I'll help him shave and everything."

"I don't have to shave yet, Mr. Heath. But one day, when I'm big like you, you can help me."

"You got it, buddy." Heath high-fived Josh.

Maddie's heart spread its wings, causing a flutter in her chest. The sting behind her eyes built in intensity. She'd once prided herself on not crying as easily as the other women in her family, but in the months since her marriage had crashed and burned, tears surprised her at times.

Heath had been an important part of her life before Mark and was becoming so again. But this time, it was different. They were adults, and her daydreams weren't just about getting his clothes off.

***

Heath straightened his tie, glad he'd brought it. He liked to dress up for his dates with Sara Ann. In his experience, girls always went to a lot of trouble to look nice, so the guys should put in a little effort, too.

Earlier in the day, he and Josh picked out flowers for their ladies. He handed Josh his and let him knock on the door adjoining the rooms. It had been open the entire trip, but they'd closed it, so they could get ready for date night separately.

Maddie opened the door, and Josh stepped inside, shoving the flowers at her without ceremony. They'd have to work on that, but it was the kid's first date, so Heath cut him some slack.

"Thank you very much, Joshua. You look very handsome this evening." She bent and kissed his cheek.

"And you look very pretty. But you look that way every day, Mama."

Points for the kid. Maybe Heath should take notes.

Maddie spun in a circle and curtsied, earning a huge grin from Josh. Heath fought to hold his in.

"You're extra beautiful tonight, Mama, 'cause you braided your hair like I like it."

Heath agreed she was beautiful every day. And since she'd gotten ready for her date, she was a freakin' super model. He had seen her in every stage of pretty, from a ponytail and bare face to hair fixed and makeup in place. In any light, gorgeous hardly scratched the surface of describing the way he saw her.

He had it bad.

"Thank you, kind sir." Maddie winked at Josh and patted her hair.

"Are my beautiful ladies ready for their big night out?" Heath asked.

"Daddy, I put on my princess dress for you." Sara Ann twirled around. "And it matches my pink fingernails."

"You look beautiful, baby girl." He squatted down and gave her a flower.

"Thanks, Daddy." She kissed his cheek before she spun in a circle on one foot and nearly lost her balance.

Heath steadied her and stifled a laugh. His brother and Anna hadn't named her Grace.

Jenny stood back a little, but she also wore a princess dress.

"And you, Princess Jenny." He walked over to her and knelt down. "I've got a beautiful flower for a beautiful young lady."

She took the flower and curtsied like Maddie had done, but with cheeks as pink as the petal of the rose in her hand. "Thank you, Mr. Heath." Jenny looked so much like Maddie at that age.

Heath looked up and caught Maddie wiping her eyes again. He averted his gaze and warred with his desire to wrap his arms around her and kiss the tears away.

"Josh, why don't you guys go ahead? We'll see you later," Heath said.

"Wait," Maddie said. "In true Katie fashion, we must take pictures." She held up her camera.

Heath laughed at the reference to Maddie's middle sister, Katie. Having been a runner-up to Miss Georgia, she was all about glamour and photo opportunities.

After several shots, Josh took his mom's hand. "Let's go, Mama."

Maddie grabbed her purse, and they headed out. Heath waited a few minutes before he took the girls.

During dinner, he worked to get Jenny to open up. Without her mama around, Jenny grew shy and reserved, much like Maddie was growing up. The exception, of course, was in the presence of family and close friends, the people she loved and trusted. It was one of the reasons Heath had always valued Maddie's friendship. He'd gained her trust, and he never wanted to do anything to lose it.

The post-dinner entertainment included a live magic show in the theater. Heath made sure Josh knew to take Maddie to a different event. Sara Ann fell asleep before it ended, so he carried her and held Jenny's hand as they walked back to the room.

"Did you have a nice time, Jenny-girl?" he asked.

"Yes, sir. Thank you for inviting me. Maybe you can take my mama on a date sometime?"

"Do you think she'd say yes?"

"If you ask real nice, I bet she'll go with you." Jenny grinned.

"What do you think? Can we get a sitter, or send you guys to the club tomorrow night, if she'll go?"

"Yes, sir. Don't worry about us. We'll be fine." She dropped his hand and skipped ahead to the door to their suite.

Before he unlocked the door to the room, Jenny wrapped her arms around his waist. "I love you, Mr. Heath."

He smoothed her hair and bent, placing a kiss on top of her head. It was the same shade of strawberry blonde as Maddie's when she was young. "I love you, too, Jenny baby."

Chapter Seven

Maddie had just put an exhausted Josh to bed and started to undress when the outer door opened. In a panic, she looked for cover and remembered her robe was in the bathroom, on the other side of the bed. She considered a mad dive and roll, but there was no way she'd get to it before she got caught with her pants down.

She looked at herself and tried not to panic. The bra and panties covered more than her bikini, but something about the lacy underwear revealed much more. At the last second, she picked up a pillow from the bed and hugged it to her chest.

Heath paused at the bedroom door with Sara Ann in his arms.

"Hey, Mama…" Jenny proceeded to share every detail of their date.

Maddie listened with interest until she noticed Heath's gaze on the mirror behind her. She glanced over her shoulder and saw he had a great view of her assets. Clearing her throat, she jutted out one hip and planted her fist on it, the pillow firmly held in place by her other arm.

He grinned and had the good grace to cast his eyes down. "I'm going to put pajamas on the little princess and put her to bed."

When he left, Maddie closed the door, so she could get into her pajamas. Then, she helped Jenny out of her princess dress. All the while, her daughter talked about her date.

"Honey, do you understand why Mr. Heath did that?"

"Yes, ma'am. He told me it's so when I'm old enough to date, I'll know how the young man is supposed to behave. If he doesn't act right and treat me with respect, then Mr. Heath said for me to call him, and he'd straighten it out. He's the sweetest, Mama. I just love him."

"I'm so glad, baby." Maddie hugged her first born. "I agree with you. He's one of the best men I know."

There was a knock. Maddie opened the door to find Heath had changed into his pajamas, too. Pants only. No shirt. Heat raced from her chest to the tight bundle of nerves seated low in her abdomen.

"I almost forgot," he said. "Will you be my date tomorrow night?"

Maddie's smile grew wide as Jenny danced around the room.

"I'd love to." She leaned against the door jamb. "But what are we gonna do about these little people?"

"It's taken care of. You just be ready at seven."

She nodded and mouthed, "Thank you." Then, stared at his butt until he was out of sight.

It's a damn shame we're just friends.

***

The following day at a Bohemian island, they snorkeled, kayaked, and played on the beach. Maddie's upcoming date with Heath had kept her awake the night before.

Jenny admitted it had been her idea, putting an end to Maddie's question of why. But now that it was on, Maddie wondered if she should take a chance and see if he'd be interested in more.

Ridiculous.

To distract herself, she checked her skin and put more sunscreen on her kids. Glad to be one of the rare redheads who could tan, she hated it for those who weren't so lucky. Her oldest sister, Liz, had the same red hair, but was much fairer.

Maddie's kids took after Mark with his light hair and complexion. Maddie had prepared for the cruise this year by visiting the Suds and Sun back home in Willow Creek. It was part tanning salon, part liquor store.

Speaking of liquor, the closer it got to nightfall, the more she wanted a drink to calm her nerves.

While dressing, she continually wiped her sweaty palms on a towel and fanned her armpits. Heath was one of her very best friends of all time, but damned if she didn't want more. She took several deep breaths and gave herself a mental slap. It wasn't like it was a real date anyway.

Unless…what if he meant for it to be a real date? A little blossom of hope swelled beneath her breast. Or worse, what if he didn't? The hope fizzled out like the bubbles in the bath she'd soaked in. Overthinking set her teeth on edge. She needed to get out of her own head.

Standing in front of the mirror, she turned to see her sundress from every angle. Did it reveal so much cleavage the last time she wore it? She wanted Heath to think she was sexy without thinking she was *trying* to look sexy for him. Was it wrong to be so attracted to him and to hope he'd feel the same about her?

Leaving her hair long and hanging over her shoulders in beach waves took the most time. Her sister, Katie, had taught her how to do it, and she'd fixed it this way for Mark once. When he didn't comment on it, she'd decided it was too much damn work to do and not get noticed.

Heath took charge of the kids and dropped them at the onboard babysitting club while she got ready. When he knocked, she took a deep breath and let it out slowly.

It's just Heath. It's just Heath. It's just Heath.

She opened the door and placed her hand on her chest in an attempt to slow the rhythm of her heart. A slow smile spread across her face as he presented her with a full bouquet of flowers. His expression mirrored hers, making his ice blue eyes sparkle. The best looking man she'd ever seen. Still.

"Thank you." She took the flowers. "You look…wow. You look wow!"

He laughed. "You're beautiful as always." He picked up a large section of her hair. "I like this. Gorgeous. Kinda like movie-star hair."

The urge to launch herself into his arms nearly overwhelmed her.

***

Movie star hair? What an idiot. But Heath had to say something. Otherwise, he'd be standing there catching flies with his mouth. He struggled not to look below her chin, where the tanned swell of her breasts screamed for his touch.

"Thank you." She patted the section of hair he'd dropped. "The fact that you noticed gives you tons of extra brownie points. Are you nervous? I'm nervous." Her words ran together like the colors on the pages of Sara Ann's coloring books.

Her admission relaxed him and he smiled. "Not anymore."

"Good for you." She turned and went into the kitchenette. "After an adult beverage, these nerves will wash away."

"It's just me, Maddie-cake." He took her hand. "Let's go out and have a little fun."

Heath had made a reservation at the adult-only restaurant on the ship. They enjoyed the Italian cuisine and shared a bottle of wine and tiramisu for dessert.

Maddie closed her eyes as she chewed the dessert. "Better than ssss…some others I've tried."

He raised an eyebrow. "How can any food be better than sex, Mad?"

"It depends on who you're having it with. Trust me, food can be way better. This tiramisu is the closest I've come to an orgasm in months. It's like a mouth-gasm." She put the last bite in her mouth.

Lord, he wanted to offer to change that for her,

but he hesitated. "There you go, making up words again."

"What? You get it right? It's an orgasm for your mouth." She sipped her wine.

He put his fork down. "I get it. Would you please stop saying orgasm? You're taking my mind into the gutter."

"Oh, come on, Heath-bar." She wiped her mouth with her napkin. "This is me you're talking to. We used to talk about all sorts of stuff, including orgasms and worse."

"I know, Mad, but it feels a little different now that we're all grown up." His mouth went dry, so he sipped his water.

"You don't…Heath, do you…?" She swallowed. "Do you want to have sex with me?"

The water he hadn't yet swallowed spewed all over Maddie, and then while coughing, he beat his chest with his fist. "What? No. Yes. No. I don't know." *You stuttering fool.*

He stopped trying to speak and used his napkin to wipe the water off of her chest. He froze when his knuckles brushed the top of her breast.

Laughter bubbled up from her, and she teetered on the edge of her seat. He caught her, holding onto her arm, so she wouldn't fall completely. It took a moment, but she regained her composure.

"Heath, I don't think I've ever seen you blush before."

The heat from his neck and face radiated like a furnace, warming their small area of the world by a few degrees.

A change of subject and scene might help. He

stood and pulled her chair out, so she could join him for the next part of their evening adventure. It was time for Maddie to be embarrassed. She didn't know it yet, but she was going to sing karaoke, if he had to carry her onstage himself.

"Uh-oh," she said when they entered the bar. "I think you planned this date a little too well, Mr. Cook."

"You've got to sing for me, Maddie-cake." He pressed his hand into the small of her back.

"Why don't we do one together?" Her pleading gaze met his.

"Like a duet? You know I like to make a joyful noise, but that doesn't mean I should."

"No, I mean, let's sing together, no back and forth. How about *Back in Black* or any of those songs we used to rock out to on our twelve-pack rides? Skynyrd, Steve Miller Band—"

"Ooh, I know…" he paused for effect, "Meatloaf."

"Noooo." She groaned. "Please no 'Paradise by the Dashboard Lights'."

They looked at the song list and settled for "Shook Me All Night Long". It was an oldie, but goodie. The crowd cheered, danced, and sang along.

When they were finished and seated at a little table, Maddie shook her head. "As much as we sang that song back in the day, I never really paid attention to the lyrics. I knew it was about sex, but darn. Maybe, it's because I have kids now, but I don't want them singing that song."

"Tell me about it. Sometimes when I have Sara Ann in the truck, I'll start singing along to the radio until I realize what I'm saying. Right after she turned three, I left her in the truck for a second. When I came back, she was singing '*hell, yeah*' along with that 'Redneck Woman' song."

Someone sang something by the Doobie Brothers, and Maddie pulled him onto the dance floor, just like the old days. Except, Heath had never been so aware of Maddie's body back then. He'd noticed it for sure, but he hadn't wanted to toss her over his shoulder and take her to bed. If he'd been more confident as a teenager, he might've tried.

After dancing to a few tunes, they went to the piano bar to unwind before going back to the room. Heath insisted he'd go get the kids, and Maddie relented at last.

At the door to the suite, Maddie rested her hand on his shoulder. "This was the best date of my life. Kinda like Senior Prom, but better because we didn't have to sneak around to drink."

Heath smiled at the memory. Both of them had recently broken up with their boyfriend/girlfriend, so they'd made a pact to go together and have a kickass time. With no relationship pressure, they'd been two friends having fun, strictly platonic.

"Madelyn Baker," he paused. "Wait. Did you go back to Baker?"

"I did. I thought about sticking with Davidson for the children's sakes, but then I said, *screw it*. We have to share our kids, but I don't have to share the name anymore." A wave of her hand dismissed the subject.

He wanted to punch himself. "Sorry I brought

it up. I just wanted to tell you, Madelyn Baker, that this has been the most enjoyable date I've been on since prom, too. Maybe, if it's not too weird, we could try it again back in Willow Creek."

She smiled and lifted onto her toes to kiss his cheek.

"You call that a goodnight kiss?" He threw caution overboard. She was too delicious not to taste.

Heat flashed in her eyes, giving him the encouragement he needed to lock lips with the girl he'd loved most of his life. He tried to keep it light and soft, but she wrapped her arms around his neck and urged him deeper, reminding him she was no longer a girl.

Just beneath the surface at every point of contact, fire burned—the all-consuming kind. Uncertainty tempered his restraint. Not knowing what this kiss meant to her, he couldn't give himself away. But a deep-seated regret for not trying it years ago bounced between incoherent thoughts.

Unsure how long they stood wrapped in each other's arms in the lip-lock of the century, he was forced back to the real world by the sound of a throat clearing.

"Little eyes on board," a woman said as she passed with kids in tow.

The teenager bringing up the rear added, "Get a room."

Maddie rested the top of her head on his chest and shook with silent laughter before she mocked, "Yeah, you horny teenagers, get a room." She lifted her head. "You better go get the little ones, before we get arrested."

Heath couldn't hide his smile. Her humor disarmed him and assured him the kiss had been right…if long overdue.

"I'll be back in a few." He gave her one last quick kiss on the lips before he turned to go. Silently, he prayed she wouldn't think too hard and regret it before he returned.

Chapter Eight

Maddie didn't pass go, she went straight into a cool shower. If she'd known Heath Cook could kiss like that, she wouldn't have waited twenty years to try it. Her body steamed up the shower before the water reached tepid. After months of being on hiatus, her hormones had awakened and screamed for relief.

This could be bad...oh, but it could be so good. It was for the best that they'd never hooked up in their younger years. Physically and emotionally, she could barely control herself now. The lack of restraint she'd had as a teenager, combined with the indisputable fact that Heath reigned as the hottest man on the planet in any decade, could've gotten her into a lot of trouble.

The cold shower wasn't helping. The more she thought, the more she craved. There was one sure fire way to put a damper on her reaction. Thinking of Mark and how they'd met. She didn't let her mind stray there long. Any time spent opening dusty boxes in the back of her brain could cause nightmares.

She toweled off and slipped on her pajamas. As she tightened the drawstring on her shorts, the outer door opened and the idea of cuddling her kids in a sweet embrace pushed all other thoughts aside.

"Mama, we're so tired." Josh wrapped his arms around her waist.

"Oh, baby, I bet you are." She swept his hair back and squeezed him close. "Go brush those nappy teeth and let's get you to bed."

Sara Ann was asleep on Heath's shoulder, so he took her to bed.

"Mama, look." Jenny pulled the collar of her shirt down to reveal red skin.

"Ooh, we missed a spot, didn't we, baby? Come here and I'll put aloe on it. Tomorrow, you can wear your rash guard shirt to stay covered."

Maddie doctored Jenny's sunburn before tucking her into bed with Josh and Sara Ann. Not wanting to be alone with her thoughts or Heath, Maddie stretched out next to Jenny for a moment.

"Did you have fun on your date?" Jenny asked.

"You bet. Mr. Heath knows how to show a lady a good time, doesn't he?"

"Yes, ma'am." Jenny smiled and yawned; mint-scented breath hit Maddie's cheek.

Heath came out of the bathroom and watched her long enough to make her squirm.

Maddie rolled out of bed and turned off the lamp. Pausing at the door, she leaned against the frame, working up the courage to tell Heath goodnight. He moved behind her, and when his body heat scorched her skin, her breath caught.

"Do you want more kids, Mad?"

She glanced up and to the side to examine his expression before she took his arm and pulled him to the other suite where they could talk. Speech would be easier if her heart would stop hammering in her ears.

She sank onto the couch, angling her body toward him. "I never wanted kids in the first place. You know that."

"How could I forget? You were the only teenage girl I knew who refused babysitting jobs. Not to mention, you were the QoC, Queen of Condoms." He propped his elbow on the back of the sofa.

"When I found out I was pregnant with Jenny," she swallowed, pushing away an unwanted thought, "I figured God wouldn't give me a kid if he didn't think I could take care of it. She changed everything. I used to hear parents say that, but I didn't believe it. I thought it was a lie they told themselves, so they wouldn't feel trapped. The joke was on me though because when that maternal thing hit me, it was all I wanted to do, and I wanted to get it right. I needed to get it right."

"Not having the benefit of maternal instincts, I was, and still am, scared to death." His blue eyes blazed with sincerity.

A man who could admit his fears. She might as well take her heart out of her chest and hand it over to him. Why did he have to be so perfect?

"It's not just maternal." She turned her head to

look at him straight on. "The Greeks call it *storge*. It's parental love, instinctual and automatic. When you see your child, who is weak and vulnerable, your protective instincts take over, and you know it's your job to love and care for your baby. You have that love for Sara Ann. She's your baby, even if she's not the fruit of your loins."

"You're right." Heath looked down where their knees bumped and swallowed. "When Glenn died, she was just over a year old, and when I held her, it was like something inside told me she'd be mine. I hadn't even discussed it with my dad. I just knew I wanted to take care of her and raise her as my own."

She reached forward and squeezed his forearm. "You're doing a damn fine job. Especially, being unmarried. I've only known what that feels like for the last eight months or so, but you've had her what? Three years?"

"Almost, she'll be four in a few weeks. The time is going by too fast." He shook his head.

"You got that right, and I hear the older we get, the faster it goes." She grinned.

A slight smile ghosted his lips. "You never answered my earlier question. Do you want more kids?"

She shrugged. "Mark and I decided two was enough, but I don't know. Maybe, if I remarry and the man I love wants more, I might do it. But not if I got too old. Don't repeat this, but when Liz was pregnant, she was a little freaked out about the increased risk of birth defects with maternal age. She called me to talk about it because she didn't want Mama to worry."

"Wait. What? Liz was pregnant? Is the baby okay?" He gripped her arm in a clench hold.

"Oh, my God, Heath. I forgot I hadn't told you about that." She covered her mouth with her free hand. "It's on the down low, so I'll have to kill you if it leaks. After Ian Clarke humiliated her in front of the world, she found out she was pregnant. She'd been told she couldn't have kids, so understandably, we all believe Ethan's a miracle from God. They're both doing great."

"Does Ian know?"

Maddie shook her head. "No, he doesn't, which is why it's such a big secret. It's her decision, and naturally, the women-folk in the family think she's right, and the men-folk think she's wrong. Ian told Liz *and* Danny on multiple occasions he didn't want kids."

Heath closed his eyes and clenched his teeth. "I'd want to know."

"I'd tell you if you were my baby daddy, Heath-bar." Even though she joked, her mind ventured to an imaginary delivery room where Heath held her hand.

His contagious laughter exploded from within. "I'd be proud to have you as my baby mama, Maddie-cake."

***

Hours passed, making Heath forget he needed to sleep. Being with Maddie had always been more fun than just about anything else. A noise from the kid's room caused him to look over her shoulder.

Jenny stood in the doorway, rubbing her eyes. "Mama, Sara Ann threw up."

He shot to his feet like a shell being fired from a gun. As he passed Jenny, he smelled it before he saw it. Her pajamas were covered in vomit.

"Oh, baby. Go rinse off and change," Maddie said. "Get in my bed. We'll see about Sara Ann."

His baby was sitting on the bed with tears falling and a hand on her belly. She didn't get sick very often, but when she did, it broke his heart.

He picked her up. "It's okay, sweet pea. Daddy's here."

"I throwed up." Her head rested against his shoulder.

"I know." He rubbed her back as he turned for the bathroom. "Do you feel better now?"

"My tummy hurts." The whine in her voice wasn't for show.

Maddie scooped Josh into her arms and checked him over. "Puke free. I'll put him in my bed and be right back."

Heath took Sara Ann into the bathroom and set her on the counter by the sink. Peeling her sullied pajamas off, he held his breath. He had a stomach of steel, but occasionally the smell of vomit threatened his steadfast control.

Maddie breezed in with a dark plastic bottle in hand. "Hey, sweet girl. Do you have a bellyache?"

Sara Ann nodded.

"Well, let's get you cleaned up and see about some medicine to make you feel better."

Thank God she was a nurse and a mom, and she had medicine. He hadn't considered any of them might get sick, which probably qualified him for the World's Worst Dad Award.

Sara Ann squatted and grabbed her butt.

"Toilet." Maddie's voice held a commanding tone of authority.

Heath picked Sara Ann up under the arms, while Maddie stripped her princess panties off. He put her on the toilet just in time.

Maddie wet a wash cloth and commandeered the trash can. "I've seen this before. Sometimes, it comes out of both ends."

Sure enough, about the time the bottom stopped spewing, the top end erupted. Most of it went in the trash can, after it landed on Heath's leg.

Maddie wiped Sara Ann's mouth then rinsed the cloth to wipe her forehead and tears. Heath stood and picked his baby up, while Maddie flushed the toilet and cleaned Sara Ann's bottom with wet wipes.

"Why don't you step into the shower with her, and I'll get a cup of water to chase the tummy medicine?" Maddie bent and turned the faucet on.

"I've got it." Heath leaned to check the temperature.

When it felt comfortable, he stood Sara Ann on the counter, so he could strip off his shirt before getting into the tub with her.

Maddie came in with fresh wash cloths and helped him clean her up. When Sara Ann was no longer soiled, Maddie took her from his arms and dried her off in the other room, while Heath removed his shorts and soaped himself down.

Barely dry, he wrapped a towel around his waist and went to find his girls. Maddie lay beside Sara Ann in his bed, singing softly and smoothing her hair back. He laid on the other side of Sara Ann and took her small hand in his.

"She drank some of the tummy medicine and is easing off a little. Jenny said she ate several slices of pizza for supper and topped it off with ice cream and all the fixings." Maddie winked.

"Thank you so much for helping me. It's much easier with a partner." He didn't care if his words sounded like a marriage proposal.

"No problem, sweetie. I'm gonna go rinse out that trash can and bring it in here, just in case."

Gratefulness filled his heart for a half a second, and then Sara Ann groaned, and her little belly echoed the sound.

When Maddie returned with the trash can, he leaned up onto one elbow. "Her stomach's making loud noises."

Maddie put her hand on Sara Ann's belly and rubbed. "She may have to go number two again. We have the can in case of emergency."

"The cleaning crew's gonna love us." He fought a smile at his sarcastic comment.

"With as many kids as pass through this place, I'm sure they've seen it all." Maddie laid down again.

"I bet you're right." The knot of unease in his gut loosened as more time passed without incident.

Heath closed his eyes, and when he woke, the sky was beginning to lighten. He still lay on his side, wearing his towel. Sara Ann slept next to him, and Maddie was on her other side with her hand resting on his girl's tummy. He rolled onto his stomach and propped up to watch them.

A few moments later, Maddie opened her eyes and smiled when she saw him. "How's our girl?" Her voice was barely a whisper.

"Still out. Thanks again, Maddie-cake." He picked up her hand and intertwined their fingers.

He didn't know how long it would take, but the future he saw for himself and Sara Ann starred Maddie Baker, his long-time friend, and he hoped one day, his wife.

Chapter Nine

Maddie spent the last full day of their cruise watching movies with Sara Ann. The image Maddie actually focused on wasn't the cartoon characters on the screen, but a vision of Heath in nothing but a towel. *Too damn hot for his own good.*

He'd taken her kids on the water rides, and that night for the grand finale of their vacation, they went on deck to watch a fireworks display.

Heath held Sara Ann and stared at the fireworks in the night sky. Maddie's kids tugged her hands and pointed, but each time she looked up, it was at Heath.

Was it too soon after her divorce to think about getting back on the horse? There must be a standard time of bereavement after a husband trades his wife in for a younger model, but damned if Maddie knew what it was supposed to be.

If Mark had died, she would take at least a year before dating or lusting after another man. As it was, it felt like a death had occurred. There was a gaping hole in her life formerly filled by Mark, and now he wasn't there. Instead, the man who stood beside her, with his little girl in his arms, had her dreaming of a life with him as her partner.

She blinked back tears and focused on the dark blue velvet sky. It must've been their proximity and the family environment that had her mind chasing rabbit trails.

The next time she glanced at Heath, his smile rocked her core. The affection in his eyes shot adrenaline straight to her heart like the jolt from a defibrillator on a dying patient.

Should she tell Heath she was falling in love with him, and she desired another soul-lifting kiss and wanted to wake up in the same bed with him again?

Stop thinking and act.

Moving closer, she snaked one of her arms around him. He reciprocated and hugged her with his free arm. Her kids stood a little in front of them.

"You have a beautiful family," an older woman said to them.

Maddie was about to explain they weren't exactly a family, and while she hesitated, trying to figure out what to say, Heath surprised her.

"Thank you. I'm a lucky man." He squeezed Maddie and placed a feather light kiss on her lips.

"Will you take our picture?" Maddie asked, holding out her camera to the stranger.

They posed as the lady obliged. They thanked her, and when the fireworks ended, they headed back to their suites.

"Mama, you're really pretty, and Mr. Heath is really handsome," Jenny said. "So, I think y'all should get married."

"Tell me how you really feel." Maddie hoped her face wasn't fire engine red as she ruffled Jenny's hair.

Her daughter rolled her eyes. "I just did. Duh."

"Here's the thing, Jenny. Mr. Heath and I would need to determine if we're compatible and in love before we got married. It's not as simple as looking good together or saying it should happen and then it happens."

"But you've already been on a date." Jenny's face held the ready-to-argue-expression she got with her brother. "He likes you a lot, and you said you love him."

"I've loved him since we were kids, but there are different kinds of love, honey. With grown-ups, it's a little complicated."

"Why?"

Heath spoke up. "Jenny, if I decide to get married, I have to love someone very much, and I have to be sure they're a good mother for Sara Ann. It's the same for your mom. She has to be in love and make sure the man is a good father figure for you and Josh—not that he would replace your real father, but he would have to love you just as much. Can you see how difficult that might be?"

Jenny shrugged. "I guess. In the whole world, it would probably be hard to find someone who loves me as much as my daddy does, but I think you're pretty close. My daddy never took me on a date before."

Maddie covered her face with her hand, hiding the shame of crying once again.

"I'm sorry, Mama."

"You didn't do anything wrong, baby. You know you can always talk to me about anything, but I think it's too soon to be talking about marriage right now. Mr. Heath and I are reconnecting after not seeing each other for a lot of years, and well…you know my heart was broken after your dad and I split up. Hearts take a little time to heal."

"I hate him sometimes." Jenny crossed her arms over her chest.

"Don't say that. He's your father, and you need to honor him. He didn't divorce you. You'll always be his little girl. He loves you very much."

Jenny poked her lower lip out. Heath passed Sara Ann to Maddie and picked Jenny up.

"I know it's hard to not be mad at your dad right now because you see how much he hurt your mom. I'm mad too, but I can't hate him because without him, you and Josh wouldn't be here. Hard times build character, and y'all are going to be stronger for having survived it. There's also this little thing called forgiveness."

He placed a finger under her chin, so he could look her in the eye. "One day, when you're ready to forgive, you'll feel like a weight has been lifted from your shoulders. Carrying anger only weighs down the person who's holding it. Do you understand what I'm telling you, Jenny-girl?"

She sniffed and nodded her head before resting it on his shoulder.

After they put the kids to bed, Maddie stepped

out onto the veranda for some fresh air. The things Heath had told her daughter hit too close to home. Especially the forgiveness thing. If she ever let her burdens go, she hoped gravity would be strong enough to hold her down.

The next day, they would make the long drive back to Georgia, and she'd have to drop her kids off with Mark for a couple of days. She anticipated the hell she would catch when Mark found out Heath and Sara Ann had accompanied them on the cruise, instead of Johnny and Nick.

She ran her hand through her hair and sighed.

"You okay?" Heath joined her on the balcony.

"Yeah, just sorry the trip's nearly over. Thank you for talking to Jenny earlier. This parenting thing is tricky. I never know if what I'm saying will ruin their lives."

He pulled her into a hug. "You are a great mom, Maddie. Give yourself a break. You've been through a rough time, not of your own making. You're doing the best you can."

She inhaled, committing his scent to memory. "Heath, the last few days…"

"Have been great, haven't they? I didn't know how much I missed you." The palm of his hand rubbed her back.

"Me either, but I have to ask you…is there something…" She let out a breath. "Is it my imagination or is there an attract—"

His mouth covered hers, both interrupting and answering her question simultaneously. She melted into him. The man knew how to kiss her troubles away.

Chapter Ten

Heath's body propelled him to take Maddie all the way, but his brain kept getting in the way with threats that he might lose her if he pushed too far, too fast. He broke the kiss and pulled back to catch his breath.

"Whew! Hot-to-mighty!" She fanned herself with her hand.

A bead of sweat trickled down his back, and he smirked. "Stop teasing me."

"Me?" Her eyebrows shot up, and she tilted her head to one side. "You planning to finish what you started?"

"Yes, but not tonight. I want to do this right. I think we have a chance, but we need to take it slow. You're not even over Mark yet."

She narrowed her eyes. "How do you know that?"

"Every time I turn around, you're crying."

"You don't know me as well as you think you

do, Heath Cook." Maddie pulled away and went inside.

He leaned against the rail of the balcony and stared at the murky ocean. His thoughts were just as unsettled as the swirling water. After a minute, he followed only to find her bathroom door closed.

He tapped two fingers against it. "Mad, don't run away from me. Tell me what's on your mind."

She opened the door with such force the wind nearly knocked him back.

"I'm so pissed at you right now."

"Why?" He stepped closer.

"Because you make me feel things I have no right to feel. Please—"

He gripped her upper arms. "Why do you think you don't deserve to be happy?"

"Because I failed, okay?" She dropped her head into her hands.

Slipping his arms around her, he softened his tone. "Maddie, don't you dare believe that lie from the pit of hell. It's not your fault your marriage ended."

"It kinda is. I suspected he'd cheated on me early in our marriage, but I couldn't prove it, and he denied it. I chose to believe him and stay with him. When I caught the bastard, he hinted that he'd been getting away with it for years. If I'd been a good wife, he wouldn't have cheated, right?"

"Wrong." He took her hands and led her to the end of the bed where he sat next to her. "Honey, listen to me. Men like him don't appreciate a good thing when they have it. One day, when he realizes what he's lost and that no other woman is gonna put up with his bull, he's gonna come crawling back to you. When he does, I hope you kick his ass to the curb."

Her shoulders shook. "You always know the right thing to say, Heath-bar."

"That's because I do know you better than you think." He placed his index finger on the center of her chest.

She looked up at him. "I haven't been crying over my own loss. I hurt for what my kids have lost. For the perfect family the Cleavers sold us that isn't real. I want my kids to believe in love and happily ever after, but I also want them to be prepared to deal with the loss if they don't find it."

"Maddie, there's a happily ever after out there for you…and for me. Some of us just find it later than others. People aren't perfect. Life throws us curve balls, and we have to roll with the punches—"

"And we have to kiss a few toads. Have you rehearsed every cliché known to man? Or are you just rolling with it?" She smirked.

"Maddie, I love you. Not just because I've known you all my life, but *love*, like the real kind." He ran a finger down her cheek and along her jaw. "I want a future with you." A bass drum beat deep in his chest. "I want you in every way."

Her eyes lit up. "Thank God."

He shook his head. "Not tonight."

The hope flickered out of her expression. "Damn you, Heath." She shoved against his chest. "Do you know what you do to me? I have needs."

"And I don't? Do you know how hard it is to keep my hands off you?" Though technically, his hands were on her. One rested on her low back and the other twined with hers. He struggled to keep them there.

"Why don't you show me how hard it is?" She leaned closer.

He cleared his throat. "You're testing me beyond my control."

"It's just me, Heath-bar. We've shared almost everything. Why not each other?" She ran her hands up his chest and latched them behind his neck.

"Because I don't want you to regret me. I don't want to lose you, Maddie-cake. I've loved you most of my life, but this," he gestured between them, "is a new kind of love. It's foreign for both of us. I'm telling you as hard as it'll be, we need to take this slow. We owe it to our kids and to each other."

"Thank God you're being the level-headed one now." She sighed and looked down. "I know you're right."

He picked up a strand of her hair and let it slip through his fingers. "You can't help it. This red color makes you a little reactive, sweetie. You know I love you anyway." He kissed the top of her head.

"All right, take those lips and go. Goodnight, cowboy." She smacked his ass when he stood.

Every cell in his body protested, telling him to go back and make a memory neither of them would forget. One foot in front of the other was the only way he made it out of there without claiming her, body and soul.

Chapter Eleven

On the trip home, Maddie let Heath drive her Suburban back to Georgia, so she could wallow in her shame. It wasn't everyday she threw herself at a man and got shot down. She should be glad he refused to take advantage of her vulnerability, but instead, the rejection stung worse than if she'd pissed off a nest of yellow jackets.

Glancing at the time on her phone, she hesitated to call her ex. The plan was to drop the kids off with him for the remainder of their Spring Break holiday. Dread took a seat in her solar plexus. Mark had no right to get upset about her vacation company, but he would anyway. *The jerk*.

She let out a long breath and leaned back against the headrest, knowing deep down she should've told him.

"You okay?" Heath asked.

She glanced at the speedometer. "Do all state patrolmen have lead feet?"

"Yep. Am I scaring you?" He gripped the wheel with both hands.

"Not me, but we do have precious cargo on board." She nodded toward the back of the car.

"You included." He reached over and took her hand.

She peeked at the backseat.

"They're all out," he said.

"I think they need a vacation from their vacation."

"So do I. How about a relaxing ride later? We can go to my place or ride at Southland. My dad wants some time with Sara Ann, since he hasn't seen her all week."

"Sounds nice. You know just what I need." *Except you won't give it to me yet.* Unfulfilled expectations were making her nuts.

They pulled up to her old house in Decatur, a suburb of Atlanta. When she thought of the time, money, and effort she'd spent fixing it up, she wanted to slap somebody.

It was Mark's house now. In the beginning, they'd done the work together. But since he was better with a scalpel than a trowel, she'd eventually hired out the big projects and recruited her family to help her with the smaller ones. Her blood, sweat, and tears went into making their house a home, and now it was broken.

Maddie woke her kids and carried Josh, while Jenny walked. Needing help with their luggage was the only reason she didn't ask Heath to stay in the car. She hadn't done anything wrong, so she wasn't going to hide Heath like she was ashamed of him.

Mark met them at the back door. "How was it?" His smile faltered when he saw Heath.

Maddie reintroduced the men, and Heath passed the suitcases to Mark.

"My baby's asleep in the car, so I'll go wait with her. Bye, kiddos."

Jenny put her arms around Heath's waist. "Bye, Mr. Heath. I had fun."

Josh reached his arms out, and Heath took him from Maddie. "Bye, buddy. Get some rest."

"Okay. See you later, alligator," Josh said.

"Maddie, I need to speak to you." Mark ushered the kids into the house.

"Here we go," she mumbled under her breath.

Heath, already on his way back to the car, stopped and turned to check on her.

"I'll be right there," she said.

"I didn't know you'd have company." Mark leaned one arm against the brick by the door. "I'd like to talk to you. Can I call you later?"

"What is it, Mark?" She wanted to argue and get it over with.

"Nothing big, darlin'. I just miss bouncing things off you, that's all."

Maddie bit her lip to keep her retort from flying out of her mouth. He really should've considered that before he threw her away.

"Look, I'm exhausted." She ran a hand through her hair. "Can we talk in a few days when I pick up the kids?"

"Will you leave the muscle-head in Willow Creek?"

She grinned at the reference to Heath. "Yeah, I

will."

"Why didn't you tell me he was going on the trip?"

"Because I didn't need your approval or permission." She let out a weary breath. "Are we done? I'm ready to get home."

He reached out and stroked her cheek. "This was your home once. It could be again."

***

If Heath thought Maddie had been quiet on the drive from Florida, he was mistaken. Something was definitely on her mind.

"What did he say to you?" Heath rested his elbow on the console, leaning toward her.

"Not much. He didn't know you and Sara Ann went with us, so he had to give me a little bit of a hard time."

"I'm sorry, darlin'."

"Don't call me that." Her harsh tone made him snap his head around.

She sighed. "I'm sorry. Mark calls me that because I told him I love that Big Daddy calls my mama *darlin'*. I was never sure if he was being sarcastic or if he actually thought of me as his darling. Either way, I don't want to be called that anymore."

"I'm sorry, Maddie-cake. I've been calling you *that* since the third grade. Is it okay?"

She fought a smile. "Of course, it's okay. As long as I can keep calling you Heath-bar when the mood strikes."

"I'll always be your Heath-bar." He winked and reached over for her hand.

After a moment's hesitation, she opened her fist and twined their fingers. "Thank you for everything. For being my friend and for respecting me enough to tell me the truth, even when I don't want to hear it."

Respect and truth-telling had led to a serious case of blue balls, but he wasn't about to tell her that. He wouldn't be the rebound guy. He wanted to be the forever guy, so he would remain steady and dependable, like always.

After a quick break for fuel and caffeine, his next stop was his dad's house, where he dropped off Sara Ann. His family, like the Bakers, had a compound of sorts.

Glenn had built a two-story, five-bedroom home with wood siding and a wrap-around porch. Situated in a dense wood, far back on their dad's property with a long, dirt lane leading to it, they had to drive past the stables to get there. With all the acreage they owned, there was still plenty of room to ride.

Glenn and his wife had wanted a houseful of kids. Heath had never really considered having a big family until he'd moved into the house with Sara Ann. He'd been living up at his dad's three-bedroom, brick, ranch-style house closer to the main road, when Glenn and Anna had died in the car accident. He and his dad had been babysitting Sara Ann when it happened.

He remembered the call and the whirlwind of soul sucking anguish. Heath had served as the Traffic Homicide Investigator for the area, but when the authorities discovered the victims were his family, they'd called in someone else for the job. Since his dad was sheriff and his friends were on the scene, they'd still been privy to every detail of the gruesome accident. Closed caskets at the funeral had been the only option.

"Do you think about them every time you drive this lane?" Maddie asked.

As he snaked her SUV down the pathway, he shivered. She'd always had a sixth sense.

"Almost." He cleared his throat. "It's not as bad as it used to be. I used to feel guilty because I'd inherited a life they were building together."

"I'm sure it was hard, but I can't see you doing it any other way." She rubbed the backs of her fingers across his cheek.

He put the vehicle in park in front of the house and closed his eyes, savoring her touch as he leaned into her hand. Maddie Baker was hard to resist. The stronger his feelings grew, the more difficult it would be.

"How 'bout that ride?" he asked.

"I thought you'd never ask." She wriggled her eyebrows then burst into giggles.

He knew better than to ask ambiguous questions.

"I want to ride Trigger." She climbed out of the SUV.

"Trigger's getting old, but he still likes to feel useful."

Heath took Maddie's hand as they walked to the barn. In the late afternoon sun, her hair glowed like molten lava. The same way his insides melted when she was nearby. With a couple of hours of daylight left, Heath wanted to make the most of every moment. When the day ended, their vacation would be over.

"It feels good to move after sitting for so long." Maddie shook out her legs as she walked.

They reached the barn and saddled two of the four horses. Heath and his dad didn't have as many as the Bakers, but they also didn't have as big of a family. Four was plenty, and they weren't cheap to feed and care for, especially on law enforcement salaries.

They rode a single track trail until they reached an open area near a small creek and were able to ride abreast.

"Do you miss it?" he asked. "The rodeo circuit, from back in the day."

"Nah, I'm too old for that mess now. I don't have the upper body strength to hold myself up trick riding. That's a sport for young'uns, which Jenny has been asking me about, by the way. I don't know what to tell her." She shook her head.

"Was it all that bad?" The leather in his hands squeaked from his grip.

"No, especially not the part where you and I became close, but it seems so dangerous now that I'm not the one doing it. I don't want her to get hurt. In fact, I'm surprised my mama ever let me do it."

"Your mama was busy with the business and six kids. I'm not surprised the danger factor went unnoticed. Besides, it was Big Dan who encouraged you, wasn't it?"

Her smile broadened. "Yeah, it was sort of our thing—the riding and rodeos. Johnny got into it a little bit, but he wasn't big on competition. He hated to lose."

"We all do, but that's a part of life. We have to learn how to lose gracefully and win with humility."

"So, are you saying I should let Jenny give it a try?" She squinted into the sun, her turquoise eyes sparkling.

"We can work with her, you and me. She can try a few things and see if anything fits. Speaking of, there's a rodeo and horse show near Dallas tomorrow, if you aren't sick of me and feel like riding over there."

"I never get sick of you, Heath-bar, and I'd love to go. I just need to check with Mama D and work, make sure all is well."

"If you can go, I'll pick you up at ten." He pulled the reigns to turn his horse and took off in a gallop.

She caught up. "I've missed this. I'm glad you're making plans with me because I didn't want the trip to end. I was afraid you'd grow tired of me."

"Never." He slowed his mount. "You're one of my favorite people in all the world. Always have been. I'm sorry your marriage fell apart, but I'm glad I have you back." He reached out and squeezed her arm.

"Me too." Halting Trigger, she turned to him. "It broke my heart when you went off to college. I missed you so much I studied my tail off during the week and partied it off on the weekends, just so I wouldn't have to think about you making a new life somewhere without me."

"And when I came home and found out you were dating a doctor, I knew it was over. No man is gonna let his future wife hang with her best friend if they're of the opposite sex. I gave up and didn't even try to reconnect after that." The sun was setting on their trip down memory lane.

"Enough talk about regrets. Our paths brought us here, and we should look ahead. I'll race you back to the barn." She clicked her tongue, and for the first time in a long time, Trigger kicked it into high gear.

When he caught up to them, Heath could have sworn the horse was smiling. He was too. Maddie Baker could always make his heart smile.

Chapter Twelve

Maddie descended the stairs in stealth mode and listened to the deep, manly voices in the living room. One in particular made her tingle in unexpected places.

Peeking around the corner, she took a moment to observe Heath as he chatted with Johnny and Big Daddy. Wrangler should hire Heath to model their jeans because they fit him like they were made of spandex, showing off the mouthwatering curve of his ass. The metal of his belt buckle glinted in the light, and her breath caught. It was a gift she'd given him years ago, double horseshoes with a galloping horse.

His solid blue button-up matched his eyes, which met hers at that moment. Beautiful. Not a word she often used to describe men. The ladies at the rodeo would drool all over him, and she couldn't blame them. She was half drooling herself.

"What are you staring at?" Johnny asked,

interrupting her plunge into Heath's eyes.

"A damn goodlookin' man," she answered before she thought better of it.

"Aw, hell. Mad, I need to talk to you." Her brother took her arm and dragged her into the rec room.

"What're you doing? Heath's a great friend to you. Don't use him to get over your broken heart. You'll lose him, and you'll regret it."

"I'm not using him." She pulled her arm away. "We're just…enjoying each other's company, rekindling our friendship."

"Something's kindling all right. I can see it in your eyes and his. Think about this. Not only how it affects you, but your kids and his." Johnny's finger pointed in her face.

"What if we're the real thing, Johnny? What if Heath has always been the one for me?" She motioned to the other room.

"I always thought you two were meant to be, but this is too fast and too soon after your divorce. Please take it slow. I don't want to see either of you get hurt." He slid his hands down her arms.

"I don't want that either, bro. I'll be careful, I promise." She kissed his cheek. "Thanks for looking out for me."

"That's my job, little sister." He patted her head.

When they were in Heath's truck on the way to the rodeo, Heath asked about her conversation with Johnny.

"It seems my immature big brother is growing up, and he doesn't want us to move too fast and get hurt."

"Us? As in you and me? I don't want that either."

Maddie grunted in frustration. How was she supposed to proceed? She wanted to be Heath's friend, but she wanted much more with him. Maybe she was being too hasty. Only the day before, Mark had stirred up some unexpected emotions in her, and she'd tossed and turned all night trying to beat them down.

Riding waves of emotion and feeling confused all the time did not sit well with her. Control was necessary for her survival and peace of mind. Although she'd been a slightly rebellious youth, she missed the order and predictability of the life she'd built with Mark. Oddly, she didn't miss Mark too much, and guilt flooded her at the admission.

They'd had sex every Saturday and Wednesday. They didn't call it hump day for nothing. There were occasional splurges on holidays or after too much alcohol, but it was predictable.

It'd been so long since she'd had sex, she'd probably get a butt cramp the first time she tried it. *That* was just how she wanted Heath to see her. She smiled at the thought because even though it was an awkward thing to have happen, she could picture herself laughing with Heath about it, totally unashamed.

"You've gone from sighing to smiling in a minute, Maddie-cake. Talk to me." Heath took her hand.

"What can I say? I'm a fickle female." At his

raised eyebrows, she continued. "The truth is I have to keep talking myself out of dark places. My mind will start down a road I don't want it to go, and I have to have a reality check and turn it around."

"I know all too well about that. After Glenn…" He paused to swallow. "There were dark days. But thanks to Sara Ann and a therapist, they gradually became dark moments like what you're experiencing now. If you ever need to unload, I'm here."

"I feel terrible that I wasn't there for you after you lost your brother." She squeezed his fingers.

"Hey, you were at the funeral. You had your own life and stuff going on. We weren't…in touch—"

"That's what I feel so bad about. I should've kept in touch. I should've let you know how much you meant to me, instead…" Her eyes blurred with tears, and she turned her head away from him, hoping he wouldn't see.

"Instead of what, Maddie? Do you think I rejected you?"

"I knew better, but it sure seemed like it at the time. I knew how badly you wanted to go to college, and that scholarship was a great thing. I just didn't realize I'd never get to see you, until it was too late. So much time had passed, and you'd moved on."

"I'm the one who should've told you how I felt. I wanted to go make something of myself, so I could come back and impress you. Instead, I came back to find you with someone I couldn't compete with."

"Heath, are you saying you loved me back then? As more than a friend?" Her heart slammed against her ribs.

"Maddie, I've loved you since the day you walked into Mrs. Simpson's classroom. You had your hair in two long braids, and you wore a plaid shirt with blue in it to match your eyes and your blue pants, which were tucked into your burgundy boots. You sat next to me and smiled at me when I told you my name. You were missing your two front teeth and so was I."

"I thought you said your name was Heesh because you couldn't make the '*th*' sound without those front teeth, but then neither could I. I can't believe you remember what I was wearing. I coveted your Dukes of Hazzard lunchbox, and we swapped sandwiches. I had bologna, and you had PB&J."

"I made that sandwich myself, and I was so proud you wanted it. I think the bread was all torn up from me smearing the peanut butter on it." His laughter took her back in time.

"The best PB&J I ever ate."

Shoot. She turned away because her eyes were leaking again.

***

Heath raised Maddie's hand to his lips and kissed it. He thought briefly about how different things might have been had he given her his heart back then. But he knew better than to play the *shoulda, woulda, coulda* game. They'd both needed to grow up and live a little. He'd always told himself if they were meant to be, they'd get their chance. This might be it, and he hoped like hell he didn't screw it up.

They were traveling west on Interstate 20 through Atlanta when blue lights in the distance caught his eye. As they got closer, he saw multiple sets of blue lights and a few red ones. Accident with injuries.

A knot formed in his stomach. It happened every time he went on an accident call.

He let go of Maddie's hand and white knuckled the steering wheel. Slowing, he moved over one lane to the left, since the emergency vehicles were off on the right shoulder.

Maddie gasped about the same time he recognized the little girl standing at the rear of the ambulance.

"I know, sweetie. Hang on." He turned on his flashers and maneuvered onto the shoulder past the scene of the incident.

Before he could warn her to be careful of the traffic, Maddie jumped out of the truck. People drove like idiots and were often the worst threat responders faced on the job.

Heath joined her at the back of the ambulance, where Jenny gripped her mom like a vice and her little body racked with sobs.

"Take her." Maddie kissed Jenny's head, then pushed her toward Heath as she climbed into the ambulance.

Josh rested on the gurney, and the medic held gauze over the child's left eye.

Heath scooped Jenny in his arms as he moved closer to hear the details. Josh had a cut above his eyebrow, which would require stitches, but the EMT didn't report any other injuries.

"Cookie."

Heath turned to see his friend and fellow patrolman, Drew.

"Hey, man." They shook hands. "What happened?"

"The driver," Drew checked his notes, "Christy Mullins ran into the concrete barrier. She was the most seriously injured. Her ambulance is already en route to the hospital. I take it you know these kids?"

"Yeah, that's their mom in there." Heath pointed. "She and I were passing by when we saw Jenny here. Where's your dad, sweetie?"

Her voice wavered as she struggled for breath. "He's on call, and Christy wanted to take us to Six Flags, so he gave her the credit card and keys to his new car and told us to go have fun."

Heath looked to Drew. "Their dad's a doctor at Emory, so I'm sure they'd prefer if Josh were taken there."

"Heath," Maddie said from the back of the ambulance, "I'm going to ride with Josh. Will you bring Jenny and follow us?"

"Of course, we'll be right behind you." He took Maddie's hand and squeezed, trying to convey comfort with one touch.

Heath got Jenny buckled into her seatbelt in the passenger seat and then paused at the back of his truck to take a few deep breaths. His heart had nearly stopped when he'd seen her standing on the roadside, but he'd forced himself to keep it together for Maddie's sake. He sent up a quick thanks to heaven for their protection before he climbed behind the wheel.

On the drive, Jenny cried so hard he thought she would make herself sick.

"Jenny, baby, are you hurt?"

With her face in her hands, she shook her head.

"You know your brother's gonna be all right, don't you? A few stitches and he'll be good as new."

She sniffed and nodded.

"Why are you so upset, sweet girl?" He rubbed her back.

"Because it's my fault." She wailed. "I caused the wreck."

He dipped his chin and cocked one eyebrow. "How did you do that?"

"I smarted off at Christy, and she turned around in her seat to look at me mean. That's when she ran off the road and hit the wall." She wiped her nose with the back of her arm.

He reached in the console and handed her some napkins. "Kids smart off at their parents in cars all the time, and most of them don't wreck over it. You can't blame yourself. You could have been nicer, but you didn't make Christy take her eyes off the road. That was her choice."

"My daddy's gonna hate me." She hiccupped.

"No, he won't, baby. He's gonna be so happy you're okay that he won't have time to get mad."

Heath wanted to tell her it was Mark's fault. His bimbo had no business being responsible for his kids. Heath bit his cheek to keep his words in check. Badmouthing her father wouldn't improve the situation. If Heath knew Maddie, she'd tear Mark a new one very soon. Heath smirked at the thought.

At the hospital, Heath and Jenny sat in the waiting room. She had eventually calmed down as he held her in his lap. She leaned her head on his shoulder.

Mark entered in a rush. "Jenny, are you hurt?" He stood her up and started checking her over.

"No, sir. I'm fine."

"She's just a little shaken up," Heath said.

"What are you doing here?" Mark straightened. "Why is it that every time I turn around, there you are—moving in on my wife and my kids? Where do you—"

"Ex-wife," Maddie said from behind Mark. "You wanna tell me why my kids were in the car with your sss—" she stopped the *s* sound abruptly, glancing at Jenny before her eyes narrowed on Mark, "girlfriend, and you weren't there?"

Mark turned to Maddie, but not before his face turned crimson.

Heath pressed his lips together, so they wouldn't turn up at the corners.

"How's Josh?" Mark went to her.

"Fine, they're about to release him. I was on my way to get him a juice and check on Jenny when I discovered you unloading on my friend. What gives, Mark? You can have an affair and a live-in girlfriend, but when I start dating, that's not okay?"

"You're dating him?" Mark asked.

Heath couldn't see his face, but Mark's hands on his hips and head shake said it all.

"Speaking of dates, how's Christy?" Maddie

asked.

"I don't know. I came straight here. They took her to Grady. My kids are the most important thing. You know that, darlin'. How could you doubt me?"

Heath stood and put his hands on Jenny's shoulders as Maddie started to cry and Mark put his arms around her. Suddenly, Heath felt like an outsider intruding on their family moment. He hated seeing Maddie in Mark's embrace, but he couldn't very well push her ex out of the way, as much as he wanted to.

"Maddie," Heath said. "What do you need me to do?"

She left Mark and walked to him, hugging him and Jenny at the same time.

"Just you being here is all I need. Thank you for taking care of my girl." She bent and kissed Jenny's head.

"My pleasure." He smiled a small smile.

"Are you gonna tell her?" Jenny asked, looking up at him.

"Tell me what, baby?" Maddie sat in a chair and pulled Jenny onto her lap.

Jenny looked at Heath for a long moment before she nodded at him, tears filling her eyes again.

"She blames herself for the accident." Heath explained Jenny's concerns to Maddie.

Mark listened in. "What did I tell you about that smart mouth, Jenny?"

Jenny leaned into Maddie's neck and sobbed as Maddie raised her eyebrows at Mark in warning.

"What?" Mark asked. "I'm just trying to get

her to respect her elders."

"This might not be the best time for that conversation," Heath said.

"Why are you still here?" Mark shouted. "Get away from my family."

"Baby," Maddie said to Jenny. "Do you want Mr. Heath to take you home to Southland?"

"No," Mark said. "She's going home to my house, with me. And so is Josh. You've had them all week. This is *my* time with them. You're welcome to come home with us, but *he's* not." He pointed at Heath.

Maddie stood and fisted her hands. "Heath, take Jenny outside, please."

Maddie took a step toward Mark, and he backed up.

Time to get ripped, you SOB. Grinning, Heath picked Jenny up and carried her down the hall.

Chapter Thirteen

Maddie took a few deep breaths in and out of her nose before she spoke to Mark. If she didn't keep her temper in check, the red hair would reign supreme, and she would make a scene. It didn't happen often, especially not in public, but when it did, people better back up.

"Mark, the kids have been through enough without us compounding the problems. We need to be the grown-ups that we are and settle this affably. Now, let's go check on Josh and see where he wants to go."

As Mark followed wordlessly, Maddie organized her thoughts, saving her arguments for when she'd need them.

At Josh's bedside, she took his hand. "Honey, do you want to go back to your dad's or come home to Southland with me?"

Josh looked over Maddie's shoulder at Mark before he answered. "Dad's. But I want you to come, too. Please," he sang the word. "Please, Mama. Just for tonight."

Maddie rubbed the back of her neck as she shifted her feet. She'd been sure he would want to go to Southland, where her mama and Aunt May would coddle him. Perhaps she should've mentioned that first, but she'd tried not to influence his decision.

A couple of good rebuttals formed on the tip of her tongue, but she swallowed them back. She couldn't say no to her baby's sweet bandaged face, which meant she was going home with Mark. She avoided looking at him because if she saw a smug expression there, she would slap him. How had she gotten herself into this mess?

"I'll go get Jenny," she said. "Mark, will you take us to Southland tomorrow? The kids have school Monday."

"Sure."

She texted Heath and found him and Jenny in the cafeteria. She explained how she'd stuck her foot in it.

Sympathetic, but unhappy, Heath asked, "What about Christy? Isn't she living there too? How's that gonna be if she comes home from the hospital and finds you there?"

Maddie had almost forgotten about the home wrecker. She squeezed her temples. "You're right."

"I'm sorry to cause problems," Heath said.

"Honey, you didn't cause my problems. You're the only sane one in the bunch." She leaned over and kissed his cheek. "Let me go talk to them again."

Maddie dragged her feet down the hallway, wishing she could run away, but her hard reality lay ahead. In the grand scheme of things, she had nothing to complain about. Both of her kids had survived a car crash. For that, she was thankful.

When she found Mark sitting on the hospital bed holding Josh, her chest tightened. Women were genetically programmed to respond with physical desire for the father of their children when the father nurtured them. *Dang biology.*

For a moment, Maddie forgot her errand. The yearning turned to loathing when she remembered. She asked about Christy, and Mark said he'd check on her.

He returned a few minutes later with the news she'd been admitted for observation due to a concussion and would most likely be released the next day.

It still stuck in Maddie's craw that she'd been so quickly replaced by the younger woman. She thought about giving Mark the night of his life to make him regret what he'd given up, but he'd enjoy it, and Maddie would just feel used again.

Loveless sex. She didn't have it in her. Plus, her heart was a hair's breadth away from belonging to another man.

***

Heath couldn't hide his disappointment in Maddie's plan to spend the night with her kids and ex-husband. Mark was up to something. Maddie wasn't normally a fool, but she'd had an emotionally draining day. Heath hoped she wouldn't let herself be sweet-talked by a man who didn't love her enough to be faithful.

As he drove back to Willow Creek, the sound of Jenny's crying rang in his mind. She'd begged Maddie to let her go back with Heath. She wasn't her dad's biggest fan, presently.

It turned out to be a good thing Maddie was a woman of her word because Heath got a call from his dad that he was needed at home. In fact, his dad had dropped Sara Ann off with the Bakers, so he could go into work. As the sheriff, his dad was pretty much on call twenty-four seven, but they were blessed to not have much crime in their county.

When he got to Southland, Big Dan met him at the truck. "Did your dad tell you what happened?"

"No, he was on his way in and said he'd call me later. What do you know?" Heath glanced at the back door to be sure Sara Ann wouldn't run out in time to hear adult conversation.

"The scuttlebutt I've heard is there's a man posing as a police officer who's following young ladies and blue-lighting them. He raped and beat a college girl last night. She was found in the ditch next to her car on a deserted road this morning."

"I hope it's not true, poor girl." Dixie joined them, hooking her arm in her husband's. "But you know Dan gossips worse than an old woman, so he's in the know." She glanced down and swallowed hard. "How are our grandchildren?"

Heath filled them in, and then asked about his girl who was upstairs in the playroom with Johnny's son, Nick. Heath walked quietly up the stairs so he could spy on them.

"You be the daddy, and I'll be the mama," Sara Ann said.

"I can't play with dolls 'cause I'm a boy. You stand still, and I'll practice roping you."

"No. You be the horse, and I'll ride on your back." Sara Ann got the bossiness gene in their family.

"Okay." Nick conceded.

Heath peeked around the corner to see Sara Ann hike her skirt up and climb onto Nick's back. He was on all fours and whinnying like a horse.

"Yah, horsey, yah." Sara Ann reached behind her and smacked Nick's butt.

Heath couldn't help but laugh, but he wasn't sure it was appropriate for his little girl to play horse with Nick. The scene was both funny and disturbing.

"Well, you finally got on a horse all by yourself, sweet pea."

"Daddy." Sara Ann jumped off her fake horse and ran to him.

The best sound in the world was when his little girl sang his name, and the best feeling was when she ran to him with open arms. He hoped he would never disappoint her like Mark had done to Jenny. That would break his heart.

He picked her up and hugged her close.

"Hey, Mr. Heath. Do you want to catch me?" Nick asked, holding up the nylon rope.

"I suppose I could give it a try." Heath set his daughter down and took the length of rope from him, checking the loop knot.

Within a few seconds, he tugged the rope and

pulled Nick close. "You want me to hog tie you, too?"

"Naw, sir, that's all right." Nick grinned.

"Do me, Daddy. Do me." Sara Ann danced around.

"One time, and then we need to get home."

Once he got Sara Ann tucked into bed that night, Heath tried to call Maddie, but it went to voicemail. He supposed he needed to confirm if the reports were true before he went around warning people. Also, Mark would be bringing Maddie and the kids back to Southland, so it wasn't like she would be alone on the roads before Heath got to see her.

A few minutes later, his cell rang. "Hey, Maddie-cake."

"It's Mark. I've got something to say to you. My daughter's too young to date, and I don't want to hear about you taking her on one again—"

"You have to understand something, Mark," Heath interrupted. "If I hadn't invited Jenny, she would've felt excluded—"

Mark cut him off. "I don't give a rat's ass. You're not her father, and you don't get to make decisions regarding her. Stay away from my kids and from Maddie. Stop calling her. She's here with me in our home for one more night."

Heath turned on his calm, professional voice, although inside, he was throwing punches at Mark's face. A few words into his stern speech, he realized he was talking to dead air. Tossing his phone onto the night stand, he ground his teeth. *Bastard*.

Chapter Fourteen

Maddie followed Mark as he carried Josh into the house they'd once shared.

"How about pizza for dinner?" Mark asked.

"Yay," Josh sang the word.

Maddie stared as they went down the hallway to Josh's bedroom. A great dad when he took the time, it was hard not to love him. The years they'd shared and the love they'd built didn't just go away.

Why hadn't she been enough? Why had Mark torn them apart?

Jenny sighed as she brushed past Maddie on the way to her room. Maddie couldn't imagine what her daughter must be feeling.

Maddie tapped on the door jamb before she entered. "Hey, baby. You okay?"

Jenny didn't answer, but laid on her bed with her back to Maddie.

"Scooch over." Maddie settled next to her firstborn. "Let me check your neck. Is it sore?"

"No, ma'am."

"If it's not now, it might be in the morning." Maddie lightly massaged Jenny's neck and shoulders. "Sometimes, the impact of a wreck jerks your head, and you don't realize it until you wake up the next day with a stiff neck. It happened to me the last time I rode the Scream Machine at Six Flags. It gave me whiplash from jerking me around." What an apt metaphor for the way her heart ached from Mark's callous treatment.

"Really?" Jenny turned to look over her shoulder. "What did you do?"

"I took some aspirin and borrowed some of Aunt May's liniment." Maddie snorted, knowing what was coming.

Jenny laughed and wrinkled her nose. "That stuff stinks."

"But it works. After a few days, I felt brand new. You let me know if yours doesn't get better, and we'll give you a liniment bath."

Jenny's shoulders shook as she chuckled.

"Seriously though, we'll go get an x-ray to make sure all is well."

"Does an x-ray hurt?" Jenny bit her lower lip and turned away.

Maddie leaned around to see her better. "Does it hurt when you go to Uncle Larry's dental office and they take pictures of your teeth?"

"No, ma'am."

"Well, that's an x-ray. So, no, it doesn't hurt."

Jenny smiled and relaxed. "I might be a dentist when I grow up. Or a professional barrel rider."

"Still on that, are we?" Maddie squeezed her

shoulders. "I tell you what, when you're feeling much better, we'll talk about lessons. Mr. Heath said he'd help me work with you. We were going to a rodeo today when we saw you."

Jenny gasped, bounced, and rolled over. "Really? Next time, can I go?"

"You bet. Meanwhile, why don't we go build a fort in your brother's room and sleep there?"

Resting on his bed with a video game in hand, Josh sat up when they entered with chairs and blankets. He immediately tossed the game aside and jumped on the bed. "Woohoo. A fort."

"Settle down there, partner. We don't need you getting another knock on your noggin'." Maddie picked him up for a bear hug. He let her hold him for a second before he struggled to get down.

They set the chairs several feet apart, backs facing, and placed a blanket on the floor in the space. They put pillows down before they draped another blanket over the chairs, creating a canopy effect.

Since Maddie had no clothes at the house, she borrowed an oversized T-shirt from Mark's drawer without asking. Then the threesome donned their pajamas and crawled under the canopy, stretching out side by side.

Their singing and laughter drew Mark's attention, and soon he joined them in the tight space. Maddie pulled the sheet over her lower half since the shirt's coverage there was minimal. The kids were a barrier between her and Mark for which she was grateful because the hot look he gave her made her nipples tighten. Her sex-deprived body betrayed her.

Maddie made herself remember Mark had never joined them in their fort before this day. As a doctor, he'd once said it was undignified to lay on the floor with his children. When her kids had complained about that, she'd told them they'd have more fun without him. Mark could be entertaining though, which he proved by making even Jenny laugh.

The intimacy and cozy family atmosphere made Maddie think about what could've been.

No way. Not happening. She refocused on something happy, wondering if Heath had made it home, and why he hadn't called. She'd left her phone in the kitchen, but getting up to get it would expose her braless, T-shirt wearing self to Mark. Sure, he'd seen it before, but he'd lost that privilege. Smiling at the rise of her inner confidence, she closed her eyes.

When the kids got quiet, Maddie drifted off to sleep, thinking about Heath riding a big, black horse.

In the sexy dream which followed, Heath's lips trailed hot kisses down her neck. She ran her hands across his chest and skimmed his shoulders; then she realized something wasn't right. Heath wasn't feeling as big in her dreams as he was in real life.

She opened her eyes to see Mark's silhouette beside her.

She shoved him away and sat up, snatching the sheet to cover herself. "What are you doing?"

"I miss those little noises you make, darlin'. I was afraid you might wake the kids."

With her heart slamming against her ribs and anger quickly replacing her fear, she glanced to where her kids had been sleeping.

"Don't worry. I put them in Jenny's bed, so I could have my wicked way with you."

"Guess what, Mark." She scooted further away. "You don't get to have your way with me anymore. You have Christy for that."

"She's not you, Maddie." His hot breath still reached her in the cramped space. "We got into an argument, and she told me to stop trying to make her be you." He took her hand. "Come on, darlin', we were good together. If nothing else, let's make sweet love once more for old time's sake. Have you forgotten what I did for you?"

Maddie lost it. Him taking credit for the inner strength she'd developed sent her one step past blinding fury, and she did what she'd wanted to do since she'd read the first text message from Christy.

She placed her foot squarely where the sun had never shone on Mark's dignified anatomy and thrust hard. His cry as he fell on his side in the fetal position gave her a glowing sense of satisfaction.

Chapter Fifteen

Heath spent all day Sunday wanting to call Maddie, but not wanting to deal with Mark. It wasn't that he was afraid of Mark, but Heath had to be the bigger man or risk losing Maddie before they had their chance. If he could wait it out, her ex would shoot himself in the foot eventually.

Just after dark, his phone rang, and a little bubble of excitement flipped in his stomach.

"Maddie-cake." The smile he wore sounded in his voice.

"Hey, Heath-bar. I need to tell you something, and I'm on my way to your house. Is that okay?"

"Yeah, come on. I was about to go get Sara Ann from Dad, but if you need to talk privately, I'll wait."

"That'd probably be best," she said. "Shit, blue lights. I'm getting pulled over. I'll see you in a few."

"Wait, Mad—" Heath dialed her right back,

and it went straight to voicemail.

"Fuck." Sweat slid down his temple while dread slithered up his spine. He called dispatch to see if any officers had radioed in. No one had.

Grabbing his gun belt, he rushed to his patrol car.

His dad called when Heath's blue lights flew past on the way to the main road. While he explained his hurry, his phone vibrated in his hand.

"It's her." He clicked over to the call from Maddie. He didn't speak, only listened.

"Show me your credentials, or I'm not getting out of the car." Maddie's voice was firm and loud.

There was a long pause.

"Not just that K-mart badge. Show me your identification."

Heath's heart beat in his ears during the silence.

"Okay, step back. I'm getting out."

"No, Maddie," Heath yelled, and then held his breath.

"Shh, get your ass over here, Heath." Maddie's voice was a loud whisper mixed with a growl.

The distinctive dinging sound of the car door being opened while the headlights were still on matched the alarm bells going off in his head. An eternity passed before a gunshot pierced the air.

His heart stopped beating while he struggled for air. "Mad." The name came out in a choked whisper.

Slamming his foot on the accelerator, he grabbed his radio. The confusion of the dispatcher grated his last remaining nerve.

"Send fucking help," he yelled before throwing the radio against the dash.

Flashing red and blue lights illuminated the rural area in eerie hues, and the closer he got, the more fervent his prayers became.

When he finally saw Maddie, he gulped in air. She stood with her pistol aimed at a body laying in the middle of the road.

He cautiously approached and surveyed the scene, his eyes unbelieving. Heath raised his sidearm as soon as he realized the body belonged to a male fitting the description of the rapist impersonating the police.

"His gun's still in his hand." The whispered calm of Maddie's voice chilled the blood in his veins.

Sirens made Heath look over his shoulder. The cavalry was arriving, so he moved to stand between Maddie and the man on the ground. She lowered her gun.

When the deputy sheriff kicked the gun away from the perpetrator and bent to check his pulse, Heath holstered his sidearm and put his arms around Maddie. Through her open driver's door, he could see she'd placed her pistol on the seat.

Her expression conveyed no emotion. Her blank stare fixated on the dead man, a stark contrast to the lively eyes he loved.

He used his hand to press her head against his chest. When she finally closed her eyes, her body trembled. Holding on tight, he tried to share his strength and absorb her shock. The ache in his throat served as a reminder of how some horrors had to be dealt with in one's own time. No matter how much he loved Maddie and wanted to protect her, this would be her battle. He'd just keep holding on and help her fight.

There would be a lot of questions to answer, but if this was the criminal they'd been looking for, Maddie would be a heroine.

On the drive to the station, Heath called Big Dan and Dixie to let them know what had happened. They called Dixie's sister, Aunt Nancy the attorney, who came to the sheriff's station in time for Maddie to give her statement.

***

Maddie rocked in her seat and scraped her tongue across her teeth. The Coke Heath had given her might have helped with her shock, but it didn't quench her terrible thirst.

When Aunt Nancy breezed in with her confident air, Maddie fought off a rising fear. If she needed an attorney, she'd probably done something wrong. On the other hand, if she'd done something wrong, Aunt Nancy wouldn't let her incriminate herself.

The medics and officers had commented on how calm Maddie seemed after having just killed a suspected rapist. Actually, Maddie sensed some of the cops were angrier that the man had pretended to be one of them. The rape bit was just an added criminal element, which would've put the man away had Maddie not taken care of it for them.

She may have appeared serene on the outside, but inwardly, she was having a come-undone. If she didn't keep her hands fisted, they shook. Her training had kicked in when she'd needed it, and a sudden giddiness made her fight a smile. She never thought she'd be grateful for what she'd been through. Silently, she thanked God for protection, and that her kids weren't in the car with her.

"Miss Baker," Deputy Larson said. "Tell us what happened."

Before she began her story, she looked to her Aunt who nodded. Maddie tried to recall important details.

"What first made you suspicious?"

"At first, I only noticed the blue lights on the dash. But when he was walking to my car, I noticed the red light on top, and that didn't look right. I hit the locks a second before he tried the handle on my door." Maddie fleetingly wondered how elevated her blood pressure had gotten.

"So, he was going to open your door instead of have you roll down the window?"

"Yes, until I didn't give him that option. I hit redial on my phone and put it on speaker, hoping Heath would hear me and come a runnin'." The comfort of his hand rubbing circles on her back made her lean into him a little more.

"Why didn't you call 911 when you suspected you were in danger?"

"Because Heath is the law, and it was easier to hit two buttons than five." She struggled to keep the snark out of her voice.

"Why did you get out of your car?"

She opened her fists and flipped her hands palms up. "He had a gun."

"So did you." The deputy raised one eyebrow.

She ground her teeth. "Big Daddy calls it my rape whistle. But yeah, I had my buddies, Smith and Wesson, with three hundred eighty calibers of punch. In most circles, it's known as the Bodyguard. I'd hoped I'd never need it, but when the time came, I was glad I had it."

"Why did you shoot him in the chest?"

Heath stood and rested his hands on the back of his chair. Maddie could sense his restless energy. It was the same vibe the horses gave off just before a show.

"I was targeting his Johnson, after he told me what he planned to do to me. My aim was off. Let's call it nerves."

Maddie heard a crack and jumped. Heath had ripped the back of a plastic chair in two pieces. The muscle in his jaw ticked, his temper mirroring hers.

When she finished answering their questions and signing her statement, her dad and Johnny were waiting. They both hugged her, and it took all of her focus not to break down.

"We're gonna take you home, sugar," her daddy said, his lips on the top of her head.

"May I?" Heath stepped to her side and put his hand around her waist.

There was no inner debate. She needed an escape from her own mind for a little while. Going to Southland wouldn't give it to her.

Chapter Sixteen

Heath couldn't speak as he drove Maddie to his house, but he held onto her hand with a fierce grip. Counting backward from a hundred, his racing heart slowed to a manageable rhythm.

Once home, he led her to his truck and gave her a boost into the passenger seat before he dashed inside to grab a small cooler and a couple of beers.

He drove them to a secluded spot on Johnny's timber property across from Southland and backed his truck to the edge of the catfish pond. He let the tailgate down, spread a blanket and they sat, drinking beer, listening to the radio as it blared from inside the cab of the truck.

After he drained his beer and crushed the can, he held out his hand. "Dance with me."

She accepted, and he pulled her off the tailgate and into his arms. He rested his hands on her hips, and she slid her arms around his neck and laid her head on his chest.

Before the song was over, they'd started something they couldn't leave unfinished. The kiss began softly then deepened into something urgent and needy. His blood heated and flowed faster through his body. She fumbled with the buttons on his shirt, and he gathered her hands in his.

"Maddie." His ragged breath revealed his desire. "Are you sure?"

"Don't push me away, Heath." The rise and fall of her chest was just as shaky as his.

He let her hands go and moved his down to her waist where he tugged her shirt out of her pants and pulled it over her head. She slid his shirt off of his shoulders and ran her fingertips across his chest, sending chills all over his skin.

Reaching behind her, he unhooked her bra. Her breasts were even better than he'd imagined.

His eyes devoured her. "Maddie, you're beautiful."

"Heath, it should be against the law to look as good as you do. Definitely the best looking man I've ever seen. I'm creaming my panties over here." Her fingers stroked down the center of his chest. "Stop making me wait for you."

He laughed. They used to joke about that all the time. "Maddie, I'm gonna show you what creaming your panties really feels like."

"Ditto." She stroked him through the denim of his jeans, and he damn near lost his mind.

He unbuttoned her jeans and pushed them down her hips to reveal lacy underwear. She kicked the jeans aside and reached for his button.

"Wait a sec." He retrieved a condom from his

truck.

Taking her time, she slid his pants down his hips.

He sucked in a shallow breath. "No fair. You're getting a two-fer, boxers and jeans."

A sensual smirk landed on her lips. "Don't blame me for having forethought and wanting to see your sexy ass naked as soon as humanly possible."

His chest pounded with the force of her compliment. "In that case…" He grabbed one side of the delicate lace on her hip with both hands and ripped it in two. With a couple of flicks of his feet, his pants landed in a heap, while Maddie used one big toe to toss the scrap of material that used to be her undies aside.

"You owe me new panties."

"With me, you won't need them." He kissed her as he picked her up and sat her on the tailgate of his truck.

She lay back, and he climbed into the truck bed, but not before taking a moment to gaze at her magnificent body in the moonlight.

"Maddie," he whispered as he hovered over her. He hesitated, wanting to be sure she wanted him as much as he wanted her.

"Heath, I need you inside me. Now."

That was enough encouragement, and he glided home. Finally, he found himself in the position he'd dreamed of since his hormones had kicked in as a teen.

Inside Maddie Baker was right where he belonged.

***

116

Maddie had always wanted to do it in the back of a pickup truck. In fact, she'd wanted to try a lot of things, but had been too afraid to ask. Sex was one of the few things in her life where insecurities got the best of her.

She squeezed her eyes shut and focused on the man she trusted with her body, her life, and her heart.

Heath was more man than she'd expected, but *Oh, hell* quickly turned into *Hell, yeah* as the first wave of pleasure rolled over her. She couldn't control herself as she bucked like a bronco with spurs in her ass and cried out in release.

"Heath." She let out a shaky breath next to his ear before she took his earlobe between her teeth.

He growled into her neck, and the intense pulse of his orgasm set her off again. When he collapsed on top of her, giggles shook her.

"Are you laughing at me?" He nuzzled her neck.

"I'm so happy I can't stand myself. I love you, Heath Alexander Cook," she whispered in his ear.

He pushed himself up onto his elbows. "I love you more, Madelyn Nicole Baker."

Being with Heath introduced her to a new reality. No fear, no doubt, only passion. The sense of belonging overwhelmed her. She finally fit. With him, she could be exactly who she was, no more faking it.

In a weird way, it reminded her of the rodeo. When you know your horse, and your horse knows you, there's trust. Trust led to something Maddie had never had in intimate moments with a man—

freedom—the freedom to close her eyes and enjoy the ride.

Maddie's heart thumped hard against her chest. "That was some serious dirt road dancing."

"Come here." In one swift, effortless move, he rolled onto his back, and she went with him. "Did you hear the song that was playing while we were doing it?"

"Doing what?" She fought a grin.

"Making love."

"You're so sweet." She brushed her fingers along his cheek. "You can call it what it was." She picked up a handful of hay next to his head.

"A roll in the hay? It was that, too. But love was definitely made, Maddie-cake. Don't try to tell yourself it was anything less." He smoothed her hair. "You know you're mine now, don't you?"

She turned away and swallowed hard, dipping her chin down to her chest. "I need to go. My kids—"

He sat up. "Your kids are safe in your parent's house. My kid is safe with my dad. You and me. We have tonight. Don't push me away, Mad. I need you."

She leaned into him, and he pulled her onto his lap.

"Heath—"

"Isn't this what you wanted, Maddie?" He brushed his lips across her collarbone.

Arching her back, she shivered and sucked in air. "Yes."

He laid them back as he kissed a hot trail down her neck. She was a wet, hot mess before he even made it inside her again.

The man was perfect. She panted as she tried to tell him, but her mouth couldn't keep up with the heights he took her body to.

"Heeee-Heeee-Heath."

She was seventeen again, a fumbling idiot trying to be a grown woman and do something grown women should be able to handle. Her nails dug into his rock-hard rear, attempting to keep him still while she came for the humpteenth time.

It was a damn shame she was thirty-two years old and could have had this when she was a teenager. Her life would've been a lot different, a lifelong orgasm. Who wouldn't want that?

As she lay there catching her breath in Heath's arms, her mind drifted to her kids. If she hadn't shared a life with Mark, she wouldn't have them. Guilt weighed heavy on her chest.

She needed to tell Heath what had transpired while she was with Mark. Facing him the next morning had been extremely awkward, especially since he had an ice pack on his groin. Their kids had been a welcome distraction, but Maddie still warred with herself about treating her ex with a semblance of decency.

She turned inward, focusing on her then unmet needs. The wet "not" dream was in the forefront of her mind and reminded her how much her body needed love.

She'd been on her way to Heath's house with the intention of getting her sexual needs met. If that didn't work, she was gonna call Mark for grudge sex. Even though she may have made him infertile with that well-placed kick, she would've offered herself to him on a silver platter…and let Christy watch, if she wanted.

Ridiculous. Maddie chuckled at herself. She talked big in her head, but there was no way she'd actually go through with it.

She'd gotten what she came for, and then some. The fact that she loved Heath, and he was the best sex she'd ever had made her spasm involuntarily.

He must've have noticed because he pulled her closer, ready again. But then, so was she. So what if she'd be waddling like a rodeo clown when the sun came up?

Hours later, the sky lightened, and she was loath to leave. "I have to go get my kids ready for school."

"Marry me, Maddie-cake."

***

Heath dressed without a word, angry with himself for putting his heart on the line. Maddie had the power to crush him, and she had.

She'd explained her reasons for declining his proposal, but they seemed insufficient. He still wanted her, all of her, in his life, and in his bed for the rest of their lives.

As he drove the long driveway toward the main house at Southland, he couldn't think of anything which might convince her to change her mind.

She squeezed his knee. "Don't be mad at me, Heath-bar."

"I'm not." He gripped the wheel tighter.

"I'll marry you one day, but it's too soon after

my divorce. You understand that, right?"

"Yeah, I get it." He glanced over at her. "Didn't you have something you wanted to talk to me about? Earlier? Before the…"

"Before I shot and killed a man," she said.

"You say that very matter-of-factly, but it's not an easy thing to accept about yourself, even if it was justified."

She raised a brow. "You speak from experience?"

He nodded, done sharing himself with her for the moment. "Are you going to work today?"

"Right after I drop the kids at school."

He gave himself a mental punch and let out a sigh. "I'm sorry I kept you up all night." Stopping the truck, he put it in park.

"I'm not." She smiled and kissed his dimple. "I'll call you later."

Heath waited until she was safely inside before he pulled away. He had been worried about Maddie having regrets, but now he was the one having them. Their night together had been a dream come true, but he was way more emotionally involved and committed than ever.

He'd surprised himself with the proposal, but it was what he'd wanted all along. Fear of Maddie not loving him like he loved her rippled through him. He was also much more possessive than he had any right to be, but dammit, she was his now.

With renewed determination, he glanced in his rearview mirror as he pulled away. His new mission was to make Maddie Baker his wife, no matter how long it took.

Chapter Seventeen

When Maddie got inside the main house, Aunt May was already in the kitchen. "Aw, baby girl, come here and give Auntie a hug. Is you all right, child?"

"Yes, ma'am. Heath and I have been talking it out." More like screwing it out, but she wasn't about to tell her seventy-something-year-old surrogate aunt about that.

"He's a good man, that Heath. Yes, sirree. You ought to latch onto him, honey child. What you want to eat?"

Maddie almost admitted she didn't have an appetite, but with all of the physical activity she'd engaged in, she needed nourishment. "Is grits and eggs too much to ask?"

"You want some biscuits, too? I got mayhaw jelly."

"How can I say no? I love me some mayhaw jelly. I'm gonna go shower and get the kids ready.

Thanks, Aunt May." Maddie kissed the elderly woman's cheek.

Despite her age, her skin was smooth and the color of milk chocolate. Aunt May had been at Southland when Maddie's mama married Big Daddy. Back then, Maddie had thought it was strange for a black lady and her husband to live and work for white people. She'd learned about slavery in school and didn't think it was a good idea.

Aunt May and Uncle Ben Hill had welcomed Maddie and her sisters into the family. They'd laughed when she told them she'd help them escape.

"Why we wanna runaway from Big Dan? He pay good, and we get benefits and the retirement. Plus, I get to do what I loves to do, cook and help raise chirren. That's all I ever wanted to do. Ain't got no chirren of my own, but between Big Dan and Miss Dixie, I reckon they got more than they can handle."

Maddie smiled at the memory.

Aunt May had always forced food on her as a kid because she thought Maddie was too skinny, which she had been. Now, Aunt May did the same thing to Jenny, always making her favorites so she'd eat plenty.

Southland wouldn't be the same when Aunt May and Uncle Ben Hill retired in a few months.

***

After Maddie dropped her kids at school and explained to Josh's teacher about his injury, she made a quick stop at the florist before she went to the hospital.

Maddie took a deep breath and knocked lightly before she entered the hospital room. A woman seated on the opposite side of the bed stood to greet her. Maddie placed the flowers next to the others before she introduced herself.

Tamryn Williams would have been beautiful if she hadn't been beaten by her attacker. As it was, she had a black eye, a broken nose and collarbone, and that was just what Maddie could see from the shoulders up.

Before Maddie had a chance to tell Tamryn and her mother why she'd come, the door opened and Heath's dad entered. He wore his uniform, which meant he was there on official business.

"Hey, Maddie-cake." He gave her a side hug and kept his arm around her shoulder. "I guess I'm not all that surprised to see you here. He deserved it, honey," he said the last bit close to her ear.

Sheriff Cook released her and stepped to the bedside. "Tamryn, I need you to look at a photograph to identify the man that did this to you. Do you think you can do that for me?"

She nodded, and her mom took her hand.

"That's him." Her voice cracked, and tears ran in crooked paths down her swollen cheeks.

"We've got good news." The sheriff moved back to put his arm around Maddie. "My girl here shot and killed him last night. He was gonna do the same thing to her, but she happened to have her gun handy."

"Thank you," Tamryn's mom said.

"It doesn't take away what he did to you, but you don't have to worry about him ever doing it again," Maddie said.

"No, but now I have to worry about running into others like him," she said.

"Not necessarily," Maddie said. "One of the reasons I came to see you was to tell you about some training that's available."

"What kind of training? I took a rape prevention and self-defense class my first semester, and it didn't help against a man with a gun." Tamryn's stare fixed on the blanket covering her.

"I had something happen to me when I was in college, too. I knew how to shoot a gun, but I didn't carry one with me back then. Sheriff," Maddie turned to face Heath's dad, "I don't know if telling this will incriminate me in the death of the rapist."

"Honey, you don't have to worry about a thing. If you were trained to take care of yourself, more power to you. It's not your fault he tried to attack you." He squeezed her shoulder.

"What happened to you?" Tamryn asked.

Maddie hadn't wanted to tell that part, especially not in front of Heath's dad. She'd never told Heath because it had happened when he was away at school and they'd lost touch. Only her family and Mark knew about it. He had been the physician on duty while on an ER rotation in med school when the ambulance brought her in. That's how they'd met.

He'd been so tender and compassionate. After she recovered physically, he'd invited her to a support group and even went with her. That was where she'd found out about Roy Rigsby—the man responsible for the training, which had saved her the night before.

"When I was in nursing school, a psych patient became fixated on me. He stalked me for a while before I realized it. I started to see him everywhere I went, like the grocery store and the dance club. He always talked to me, and I tried to be nice. You know, here in the South, we're all about politeness. Even with alarm bells going off in my head, I was still polite."

"I know what you mean," Tamryn said.

"Thanks to that experience, I ain't as sweet as I used to be. Always trust your gut. Many women have gotten into trouble because they ignored their instincts and gave way to manners."

"That man," Tamryn said. "Did he…?"

Maddie stared at the floor for a long moment. "He'd gotten to know my routine and my roommate's too. One morning, Andy, my roommate was running late, and when he opened the door to leave, Walter Braddock was standing there pretending to have a flower delivery for me. I was in my room getting ready when Andy yelled for me to come get my delivery because he was running late."

"You had a guy roommate?" Tamryn asked.

"Yeah, we were in nursing school together. He's gay. When I came out of my room, Andy was gone, and Walter had closed and locked the front door." Maddie shuddered at the memory. "It was the longest day of my life."

The sheriff rubbed his hand up and down her arm. She couldn't believe she was telling this story in front of him. But he was a cop and had seen people in their darkest valleys.

"I didn't have a gun with me, and my brother had taught me some basic self-defense, but like you, it was useless in that situation. He duct taped my mouth shut and then bound my wrists together above my head. He told me he'd tape my feet to the footboard if I didn't open my legs for him. I didn't want to be any more tied down than I already was, so I did what he said."

Maddie paused and took a deep breath before she turned to look at the sheriff. "That's why I quit roping. I knew what it felt like to be bound, and I didn't want to do it to another creature after that."

"Honey, I'm so sorry. I take it Heath doesn't know about this?"

Fighting tears, she shook her head. He would go ape shit when he found out.

"Who's Heath?" Tamryn asked.

"My son," the sheriff said. "And Maddie's best friend."

"Why wouldn't you tell your best friend?" Tamryn asked.

"We only recently reconnected, and it's not something I want him to think about when he sees me. I'm not a victim anymore, but I think he'll see me that way. I don't want his pity."

"Honey, you're a survivor. That's how Heath will see you. He loves you."

Maddie nodded. "I know he does."

She turned her attention back to the young lady. "The physical recovery didn't take near as long as the psychological. I got some training, which helped me slowly put my life back together. I went from feeling like I had no control over what happened to me to having a little control. Every day, I got a little stronger."

Maddie pulled Roy's card from her pocket and handed it to Tamryn.

"Victim No More," she read aloud.

"Roy Rigby's wife and daughter were brutally attacked. His wife was killed, but he helped his daughter recover the only way he knew how, with his combat training and experience. When you're ready, call them."

"Is it very expensive?" Her mom asked.

Maddie cleared her throat. "I'm sponsoring Tamryn. In a few years, when you're living a happy, successful life and old Roy crosses your mind, call him up and offer to sponsor someone."

"Like paying it forward?" she asked.

"Exactly." Maddie let a small smile pass her lips.

The sheriff walked Maddie to her car. "Heath told me he proposed. I'm not surprised you said no. It wasn't the most romantic thing I've ever heard."

"He told you about…" Maddie swallowed hard, "that?"

"Honey, I'd love nothing more than to have you as my daughter-in-law. I think the world of you. But you know Heath can be impulsive. Maybe next time, he'll plan better and maybe you'll be ready to say yes."

Maddie fumed on her way to work. Heath had some explaining to do. She hadn't told a soul about their night, and it seemed the sheriff now knew *all* of her dirty little secrets.

Chapter Eighteen

Heath took an early lunch and went to the mall, wishing he could be invisible. He hated going into Victoria's Secret. There were rarely any other men in the store, and the women who worked there swarmed him.

"Can we help you find something?"

"No, no thanks. I'm just looking for p-p—" He picked up a random pair of women's underwear from a table overflowing with the lacy garments. "These will do."

"What style does your lady like? Cotton? Lace? Bikini? Hip-hugger? Thong?"

"Who knew women had so many underwear options?" he asked. "Men have three choices— briefs, boxers, or the newly popular combo, boxer-briefs."

"Men have bikini briefs and thongs. I bet you'd look great in both." The woman with extremely long lashes fluttered her eyelids.

He leaned closer to see if she had something in her eye, and she grabbed his arm and squeezed.

He puffed out his cheeks and extricated his arm. "My girlfriend wears lacy panties." *And she'd stomp your ass into the ground if she saw you flirting with me.* "Bikinis, not butt floss. Her words, not mine."

As he walked toward the mall exit, he tried to conceal the little pink bag.

"Heath Cook."

Dammit! He turned to see a blast from his past. Carla Peterson stood wearing tight jeans tucked into cowboy boots.

She swished her hips as she walked toward him then gave him an unwelcomed hug. "Damn, son. You fill out that uniform very nicely. If I'd known you were still gonna be so fine after all these years, I never would've married Bart." She winked. "We're divorced now, just so you know."

"I heard. I ran into Bart a few months ago at Mason's." Annoyed, he rested his hands on his belt, all the while attempting to hide the bag.

"I've been known to grace the doors of Mason's from time to time. I'll let you buy me a beer the next time I see you there, and we can catch up. Unless…" She leaned and raised her eyebrows at the pink sack. "You're not into wearing ladies underwear now, are you?"

"Ha-ha, Carla. You were always a kidder. I've got to run." Heath took longer than normal strides to get away from that regret.

If Maddie ever found out he used to date Carla, she'd be very unhappy. They'd been rivals in their rodeo days. When Heath went away to college, he was surprised to see Carla on campus. She, too, competed on the circuit, and they'd started spending time together.

The world's best blow job led to their *dating*. He used the term loosely because she wasn't too particular about who she blew, which he discovered when he caught her with Bart. It hadn't exactly broken Heath's heart when Carla quit school and married Bart. He'd only been trying to keep himself from missing Maddie so much.

Nine months later, Bart Jr. was born and Heath completely freaked out. His consolation was he'd used a condom every time he was with Carla, so unless that one percent ineffective thing happened, the kid belonged to Bart. It also helped that Bart later bragged to Heath about the unprotected sex he'd had with Carla saying *he'd rode her six ways to Sunday*. He also called her a thoroughbred, which made Heath gag a little.

Thinking about sex, he almost missed the florist. He hit the brakes and left some rubber on the road.

Condoms made him think of Maddie. She'd been the queen of safe sex in high school. Not that she had a lot of it, but she always had condoms and gave them out to him and their other friends.

"If you're gonna have sex, do it responsibly," she'd say.

Maddie had strong feelings about abortion after driving a friend to a clinic when she was sixteen. She'd told Heath everything about it, except for who the friend was. At the time, he'd suspected it was her. But when he asked, she told him she was still a virgin, and he believed her. It had taken every bit of his sixteen-year-old self-control not to offer to be her first. But he'd also wanted to be her last, and that sensation was too much for his young brain to process.

Now that he'd been with Maddie, there would be no turning back. He needed to talk to her and apologize for the world's lousiest marriage proposal, if he got to see her at all. His lunch break was almost over.

At the corporate office belonging to the Baker family home health business, Heath hid the pink Victoria's Secret bag, which had been stuffed with pink tissue paper, behind the vase of wildflowers he held. With his gifts clutched to his chest, he approached the secretary. "I'm here to see Maddie Baker."

"Maddie's not in, but I can put the flowers on her desk." The woman reached out her arms.

"Cookie Monster," Johnny called from down the hallway. "You didn't have to get me flowers for keeping my sister out all night."

"They're not for you, Shake and Bake." Heath gripped his offerings tighter, and the tissue paper made a loud crinkle noise.

"I figured as much." He waved his hand. "Come on. I'll take you to her office, and you can leave them on her desk."

Heath definitely didn't want her brother to see the pink bag. Johnny would give him hell, and Heath couldn't very well explain that he owed Maddie replacement panties for the one's he'd ripped off her the night before. This had been a bad idea.

Since he'd become a dad, he'd tried really hard to think through his decisions and not act impulsively. With Maddie, he forgot all that and reverted to his old self, where he reacted before he thought about the potential consequences.

Oh well, it was too late to make tracks for the door. He and Maddie were adults, and if Johnny said anything, Heath would tell him to mind his own damn business.

Johnny opened Maddie's office door and flipped on the light. Heath walked past him and placed the vase on the corner of her desk, while nonchalantly stashing the little pink bag on the other side of it, out of Johnny's line of sight.

"Where's Maddie?" Heath straightened. "She told me she was coming in after she took the kids to school."

Johnny eyed the bag before he answered. "I don't know, man. She probably needed to catch a few Zs since somebody kept her out all night."

A change of subject was in order. "It's strange to see you here in khakis and a polo," Heath told Johnny. "You look like a fish out of water."

"I am a fish out of water," Johnny said. "I'd rather be working outside than behind a desk. I'm trying to get Mad to take on my workload, so I can take over the care of Southland when Uncle Ben Hill retires. Work my timber land."

Heath's face warmed. He and Maddie had been on Johnny's timber land the night before.

"Why do you look guilty?" Johnny crossed his

arms over his chest.

Heath rubbed the back of his neck. "I'm asleep on my feet. Have you spoken to her? Was she okay after last night?"

"We talked this morning. She seemed all right, and she was going to see Braddock's victim in the hospital."

"Who's Braddock?" Heath asked.

"I meant Darby." Johnny scratched his head and sweat beaded on his lip. "His name was Chip Darby, wasn't it?"

Now, who looks guilty? "Yeah." Heath narrowed his eyes. "Maddie went to see the Williams girl in the hospital?"

Johnny nodded. "I hope seeing her will make Maddie feel justified in her actions."

"I hope so, too." Heath stared at the floor a moment, unable to imagine how Maddie was coping. "I've got to get back to work. I'll see you later."

From the car, Heath called his dad. "You ever heard the name Braddock before?"

"That's something you need to talk about with Maddie. Be patient with her, son. She's had an emotional day."

"Did you see her? Was she okay?" Heath cringed at the panic in his own voice.

"She's fine. I ran into her at the hospital."

When Heath got to his desk, he used the state's resources to research Madelyn Baker and Braddock. Frozen in place, his blood turned to ice.

Chapter Nineteen

By the time Maddie got to her office, her body's fuel tank was on E. The caffeine and mayhaw jelly from breakfast had ceased to keep her energized as of a few miles back. The lack of sleep, as well as the emotional trauma of seeing a battered Tamryn and reliving her own attack, had caught up with her.

As she opened her office door, flowers caught her eye, and a hormonal surge heated her entire body.

Heath. She closed her eyes and revisited their time together, imagining his arms around her.

"You made it," Johnny shouted from down the hall. The man was never at his desk.

Scooping up the Victoria's Secret bag, she stuffed it into her oversized purse just as Johnny entered.

"You look worse than Heath did when he stopped by to give you flowers and underwear.

What happened? Did he tear your panties off or something?" Johnny placed his hands on his hips.

She raised her eyebrows and burst into laughter. "Yes."

"I didn't want to know that." He covered his eyes with one hand as if he wanted to un-see it in his mind.

"You shouldn't be so nosy then, brother mine." She grinned. "Can you do me a favor?"

"I'm not returning those to the store for you." He pointed to the bag peeking out of the top of her pocket book.

"Will you pick the kids up from school for me? I need to get some work done and take a nap."

"Sure thing, little sister." He pulled her into a side hug. "I know I said it this morning, but I'm proud of you for kicking ass and taking names. The world needs more strong women like you."

"Thanks." She looked down. "I think."

Johnny knew all about her past, and he'd been very supportive. He'd always defended the kids at school who were bullied, and he got a bee in his butt anytime he heard about a woman being abused, physically or otherwise. Her dad and brothers were all protective, especially after what had happened to her, but Johnny was the most. He'd cussed and thrown stuff at first. Then, he'd calmed down and helped her find a new normal. He'd even volunteered at *Victim No More* and let Maddie beat him up.

"I love you, brother." She rested her head on his shoulder a minute.

"I know. You can't help it." He chuckled and

pulled away. "I love you, too. I'm here if you need to talk. And don't worry about the kiddos. I'll keep an eye on 'em."

After he left, she got to work.

When her eyes started to cross, she prepared to leave, but first she contacted the hospital and made arrangements to pay for the portion of Tamryn's hospital bill insurance wouldn't cover.

On the drive to Southland, Maddie sang at the top of her lungs to stay awake. Once there, she parked her SUV in the garage and jumped on the nearest golf cart. If she could make it to the guest cottage before anyone saw her, she could sleep for a few hours.

Before she took off, she inhaled deeply through her nose and exhaled slowly through her mouth. As she gripped the wheel with increasing pressure, she tried to force the images of dead men and splattered blood out of her head.

She closed her eyes, but it didn't help.

"Maddie."

At the sound of Mark's voice, she blinked several times and then lost it, burying her head in her hands. His arms slid around her as he scooted her over in the seat, so he could take the wheel.

"It's okay, darlin'. You're okay. I heard about what happened." He kissed the top of her head. "You need some rest."

She struggled to control her emotions and catch her breath as he drove them to the cottage. Her shaky stomach threatened to turn upside down. Once inside, he pulled back the covers, while she kicked off her shoes. She climbed into bed, and he lay beside her. She didn't have the will or the strength to object.

Mark was familiar. He had been with her from the beginning of her healing, and he'd helped her along the way by loving her and teaching her to trust again. He'd never pushed or demanded anything from her, but he'd waited patiently and held her hand through the good days and the bad ones.

Somehow, being in his arms now, even though he'd broken her heart, offered comfort. Instead of pushing him away, she let him hold her until she cried herself to sleep.

***

Heath ran around the front of his truck. "I'm sorry I'm late."

Sara Ann waited on the sidewalk outside of her preschool with her teacher, Ms. Becca. He'd gotten caught up in reading every report he could find about Maddie's attack and lost track of time. The lunch he'd eaten at his desk kept promising to reappear. He needed to see Maddie, so they could talk.

Why hadn't she told him? It was personal, but they'd been very close before it happened. He wished she'd reached out to him, but he also recognized it wasn't about him. He would be the one to reach out to her now and offer her the comfort and support he'd never had the opportunity to give her.

"You make that uniform look great," Becca said.

He blinked. Was she flirting? "Uh. Thanks."

He buckled Sara Ann into her car seat and closed the door.

"You know, if you ever need anything…" she touched his arm, "I'm available to babysit, or listen if you need an ear."

"Thanks, Becca. Gotta run. I apologize again for being late." He took extra-large strides to get around the truck.

"You can make it up to me." Her voice pitched high as she trailed behind him. "Let me make you dinner. Friday night?"

Geez, lady. Desperate much? I'm taken—sort of. "Um…I don't think I'm free. Bye." He hopped in and drove away before he'd clicked his seatbelt into place.

"Hey, Daddy. I love you." Sara Ann's sweet voice calmed the storm, which had been raging in him since he'd discovered Maddie's secret.

Further down the street, he pulled over and got out. He picked his little girl up in his arms and hugged her tight. "I love you too, precious baby girl. I always want to be here to protect you."

"Daddy, you're hugging too tight." She squirmed.

"I'm sorry, baby." He loosened his grip and kissed her cheek.

"What's wrong, Daddy? Your eyes are wet." Her little finger traced his cheek.

"Nothing's wrong, sweet pea. I just love you so much." He rested his forehead on hers.

In that moment, Heath knew he needed to talk to Big Dan before he spoke to Maddie. Her dad would know best.

Heath took Sara Ann home, made their dinner, and put her in the bathtub before he called Maddie's father. After explaining what he'd learned and how, Heath didn't like the advice Dan gave him.

"Let her come to you, son. If you push her to talk about it and rehash those painful memories, she won't like it. Go easy with her. Mark's making a move to get her back, and you may wind up pushing her back into his arms."

"What? Are you serious? Is Mark there now?" His voice sounded like Becca's.

"Yeah. He put her to bed in the guest cottage and is helping the kids with their homework as we speak—playing the dutiful father. Don't get me wrong, he loves his kids, but he'll use every resource at his disposal to win Maddie back. He's realized what he lost."

"Dammit, Dan, I can't let that happen." He squeezed the phone tighter in his grip, his pulse pounding in his head.

"It may help you to know how she met Mark."

Heath deflated as Dan filled him in on the details of Maddie's recovery and the role Mark played in her life during the aftermath. For the first time, Heath saw Maddie's history with Mark, their relationship, their life together from a viewpoint other than Maddie's broken heart.

"Thanks for telling me, Big Dan." He ran his hand through his hair. "I've got a lot to think about."

"Some advice from a Baker to a Cook, you can't unscramble eggs." Big Dan let the words hang in the air before he continued, "You hug that baby for me and come see us when you can."

When Heath put down the phone and returned his gaze to Sara Ann, she held up her hands as suds ran down her arms.

"Daddy, my fingers are all wrinkly."

He wrapped a towel around her, and she shivered in his arms.

"We let the water get too cold, didn't we, sweet pea? Come on, let's get some warm pajamas and snuggle under the covers."

Heath cuddled his daughter in his arms, while she sang the lullaby she'd learned from Maddie.

He knew he couldn't undo the past, but for Maddie's sake, he damn sure wanted to try.

But, how could he compete with the connection she shared with Mark?

Chapter Twenty

When the weekend arrived, Maddie looked forward to meeting Heath for a drink at Mason's. They hadn't talked all week, other than a few text messages.

She'd thanked him for the flowers and panties. He'd asked if she was okay. She told him about the rodeo on Saturday and asked if he and Sara Ann wanted to go with her and the kids. He'd replied that he'd let her know, but he hadn't.

In truth, she'd missed Heath, but she'd needed the time to get her head together. In the past, the men in her life had been crutches. Now, she was strong enough to rely on herself, and realizing it made her ready to take the next step.

Her parents were babysitting, and as she rode with Johnny to the bar, she hoped Heath would offer her a ride later—and not just in his truck. She hadn't stopped thinking about their night together, and now that she'd experienced what love could be like with him, she wanted more. She wanted it all.

A few cars passed them going the opposite direction, driving a little too fast for Maddie's comfort. Headlights reflecting on the dust in the air made it difficult to see. Mason's Jar Bar was on a dirt road in the middle of nowhere.

"Something must've gone down," Johnny said.

They arrived at the bar and paid the cover charge at the door. The bouncer had tried to wave them through, but they'd insisted. Mason had to make a living and pay his people.

A band Johnny used to play in provided the soundtrack to a good ole Southern night. Maddie knew most of the guys in The Regulators because she occasionally sang a song or two with them.

"Y'all just missed the action." Mason handed them each a Mason jar of draft beer and refused their money.

"What happened?" Maddie put the cash in the tip jar.

"The Daltons got into it with some of the Bailey boys over a woman. Chuck Bailey hit Ricky Dalton in the head with a wrench and split him wide open."

"Oh, hell," Johnny said.

"Is he okay?" Maddie asked.

"I hope so," Mason said. "Amanda Cooper was here, and she put Ricky in her car and took him to the hospital."

A visible shudder ran through Johnny. Amanda was nuts and had dated Johnny because she was obsessed with their older brother, Danny. The relationship had ended with guns, threats, and a short stint at the loony bin for Crazy Cooper.

Maddie put her hand on Johnny's shoulder. "Maybe she's got someone new to stalk."

"Ricky would probably like it," Johnny said, eyes wide.

"Damn sure would." Maddie nodded.

"I guess it's a good thing she's gone 'cause of the restraining order and all," Mason said.

"Can't believe they let her out of the treatment facility." Maddie's head shake was matched with agreeing nods from the boys. She knew all too well about delusional psychosis.

"The Baileys took off." Mason wiped the bar with a white towel. "I don't know what we would've done if Heath hadn't been here to help break up the fight."

"Where is he?" Maddie slammed her beer down and looked around the bar. "Is he okay?"

"Yeah. He had a change of clothes in his truck, so I told him to go shower at my place. Go on back there, Maddie. I know he'll be glad to see you." Mason winked.

Maddie took her beverage and walked out the back door to Mason's trailer, which sat about fifty yards behind the log cabin style bar. With music vibrating the ground, she went in the front door, her feet practically gliding toward the man she loved.

She stood at Mason's bedroom door and blinked, attempting to rid her mind of the awful image before her. The light feeling was suddenly replaced by heaviness as her lead-filled heart landed on the floor.

It wasn't the round bed or the tacky colored

fluorescent lighting that ruined her fantasies of catching Heath with his pants down.

It was the sight of a naked Carla Peterson with her legs wrapped around him.

***

"What the hell, Carla?" Heath pushed her off of him.

When he'd walked out of the bathroom to get the clothes he'd left on Mason's bed, she'd jumped him, wearing nothing but her birthday suit. It wasn't the first time. In college, it was her favorite way to *surprise* him. Apparently, she was trying to regain her youth.

Heath didn't want to body shame anyone, but Carla had always been thin, although not exactly in shape. Now, things jiggled in unflattering ways with very little muscle tone between the flesh and bone.

"Don't pretend you haven't missed me, Heath." She licked her lips and stared south of the border. "I've certainly missed you."

"Forget it, Carla. You chose when you picked Bart, and I've moved on." He used both hands to cover his goods.

"Oh, sweetie, you can't still be mad about that. It's water under the bridge. Now get over here and give me what I want." She leaned back and let her knees fall open.

Heath took a step toward her, but his next step moved him to the side, so he could get his clothes, which were next to Carla on the bed. She reached for him as he backed into the bathroom, where he closed and locked the door.

In hindsight, locking the door when he'd come

in would've been smart, but he hadn't expected to get molested. He should've had more forethought because Carla had been flirting hard ever since he'd walked in the front door of Mason's. He'd been glad for the fight, so he'd have something to do besides dodge Carla and wait for Maddie to arrive.

He checked his phone. She was supposed to have been there by then, but there were no messages from her. On the way to his truck with his duffle bag, a crying woman caught his attention. He followed the sound, but a car with booming music pulled up, and he lost the trail. He looked around a few cars in the area and noticed Johnny's truck.

He couldn't wait to see Maddie. He'd missed her like crazy, but he'd tried to give her space. He wanted her to come to him. He tossed the bag in his truck and refrained from sprinting for the door.

In the bar, he found Johnny and Mason sipping Southern Comfort.

"Y'all are gonna be hurtin' in the morning." Heath slapped Johnny on the back.

"Just getting our buzz on, bro." Johnny clamped his hand in a middle five shake, followed by a traditional grip.

"Where's Maddie-cake?"

"She went to look for you, Occifer. You panty-ripping mongrel you." Johnny grinned.

"What?" Mason asked, and then shook his head. "Never mind."

"Trust me, you don't want to know." Johnny stared at his glass.

"I sent her to the trailer," Mason said.

"When?"

"Ten or fifteen minutes ago."

"Oh, God." Heath closed his eyes.

His thoughts went to the crying he'd heard, and he hit the front door and ran for the parking lot calling her name.

"Hey, Heath. You lookin' for Maddie Baker?" A guy called from the back of a pickup truck, but Heath couldn't see who it was. "She caught a ride home. Said she was feeling sick."

Heath was getting into his truck when Johnny caught up to him.

"What up, Cookie Monster? You piss my sister off?"

"I think she might've seen something and misunderstood. I need to find her and explain." Heath was losing valuable time.

"Go get her, big dog. She's in love with you. I think she always has been." Johnny stumbled back.

Chapter Twenty-one

On the ride to Southland, Maddie swallowed the bile rising up her throat. It hadn't occurred to her to make a scene, like she had when she'd spied on Mark and Christy and caught them in the act. Their text messages hadn't been quite enough proof for her. The old saying "Seeing is believing," certainly had held true. Still did.

Heath hadn't even known she was there. Men. Throw a naked woman in their path and they could easily forget their vows and promises of enduring love.

Maddie had asked an old friend from high school to drop her at the driveway to Southland, insisting she wanted a long walk to clear her head. Holly didn't ask many questions. She'd always been cool like that.

As she walked, Maddie heard a vehicle approach, so she stepped off of the driveway and into the woods, glad she'd worn dark colors.

Heath's truck zoomed past, kicking up dust. She'd expected him to come, but she didn't want to see him. Every man in her life, except her dad and brothers, had disappointed her. She'd been wrong in thinking she was ready for another relationship.

She moved deeper into the woods and found a horse trail to follow toward the house. It was dark, but the nearly full moon occasionally showed through the thick trees, giving her just enough light to find her way. The woods around Southland had been scary when she was young, but after years of running, playing, and riding with her family, they were where she felt most at home.

Her phone vibrated against her butt, so she ducked behind a tree to confirm what she already knew. Heath's photo lit up her screen. Right after she let the call go to voicemail, her dad texted her.

She ignored Heath's message and responded to her dad.

I'm fine. Want to be alone. Tell Heath to go away.

That was a mistake because it gave away her location. Moments later, Heath traipsed through her woods with a flashlight, calling her name. "Maddie, it's not what you think."

His voice had always held a timbre which vibrated her internal organs—sexy and comforting.

She smiled to herself and leaned against a tree as he got closer. He'd definitely have to work for it. Mark would never walk in the woods at night to look for her…well, maybe if he was looking for her dead body.

She closed her eyes as Heath swept the beam

of blinding light across her face. "Maddie, thank God." He hugged her and kissed the top of her head. "I was so worried about you. Why don't you want to talk to me? Why did you run?"

"I didn't want to interrupt your reunion with Carla." She was still steamed about it.

"It wasn't…wait." He pulled back to look at her. "Reunion?"

"Yeah. I know you dated her in college." She watched his reaction in the glow of the moon.

"How?" He squeezed her upper arms.

"Because I called you and she answered the phone. She was happy to inform me I'd been replaced." A knot formed in Maddie's throat, and she looked down.

"When? When did you call me?" His grip tightened.

"When I needed a friend—" Her voice broke, and she turned her head away, hoping he wouldn't catch the tear rolling down her cheek.

He caught it in the pale light and wiped it away. "She lied. You're irreplaceable, Maddie Baker. I'm sorry I wasn't there for you. If I'd known—"

"It was for the best really." She forced herself to meet his gaze. "I needed to learn to survive without you."

"But it was hard just surviving each day." He swallowed audibly. "Wasn't it?" Heath's hands moved to her back, and he pulled her closer to his warm chest.

Maddie nodded because she couldn't speak. She rested her cheek against him and breathed him in, enjoying the feel of his strong arms around her. She wanted to put the past behind her, but if she didn't talk to Heath about it, it would come between them more than it already had.

***

They were on the verge of something big in their relationship, and Heath wanted to encourage Maddie without scaring her off. "You want to go down to the lake and sit on the dock?"

"Okay."

He took her hand. "You want a piggy back ride?"

"One woman's legs wrapped around you per twenty-four hour period should be enough." Her tone could've stopped a stampede.

"I was ambushed."

"She impaled herself on your penis forcefully then?" Even in the dark, he could sense her expression.

"She wasn't…we weren't. You must have seen the instant she jumped on me. I swear nothing happened. I don't want Carla. I'm not in love with her." He slid his arm around her.

"Mark says he's not in love with Christy either, but that doesn't keep his snake out of her garden."

His muscles tensed and he held his breath. "I'm. Not. Mark."

"Cut me some slack." The tightness in her posture matched her voice. "Every insecurity I've ever had in my life has been rehashed this week, including seeing you naked with Carla." She pushed his arm and walked away from him. "You know what? Forget it. This was a mistake."

"Wait, Maddie. I'm sorry I got angry. This week hasn't been a cakewalk for me either, but being compared to Mark, even when the evidence said otherwise… Maddie, I would never do that to you." He gripped her upper arms in his hands. "I hope you know me well enough to believe that. I know how much his actions hurt you. I never want to harm you. This…we…are *not* a mistake."

"It was too soon. You tried to tell me, but I wouldn't listen. I was being selfish, and I'm sorry. I don't want to hurt you either, but now, everything has changed."

"Because we made love? Maddie, it was perfect. Why are you trying to make it less than it was?"

"I don't mean that. I mean things are different now because you found out what happened to me, and you see me differently."

"Where do you get off telling me how I see you?" It was his turn to raise his voice. "If you see yourself differently, as a weak, scared, little woman, then own that."

Maddie looked at him as if she were seeing him for the first time. "You're right, Heath. I didn't want you or anyone else to know about my past because I was afraid they'd see me the way I do sometimes—as a weak, scared, little woman."

"You aren't those things, Maddie. Woman, yes. But not the others."

"Are you calling me fat?" She put her hands on her hips.

"What?" His alarm faded when he saw her smile. "You know good and well you aren't fat.

You may have weak moments and scared ones too. But you're a strong, beautiful woman, Maddie Baker. *Every* moment of your life. Get that through your thick head." He tapped the center of her forehead with his finger.

"Are you doing the tough love thing? 'Cause it's totally working for me."

"Somebody's got to keep you in line."

She slid an arm around his waist, and he slung his around her shoulders. They continued their walk past the main house down to the lake. Once there, she got blankets from the storage locker, and they made a pallet on the dock.

They laid back, and Heath watched the night sky as Maddie told him about her attack. The fear and apprehension he'd experienced when reading the reports came back full force. He battled the negative and focused on Maddie, on her strength. Impressed by the training she'd received, he asked a lot of questions.

"What went through your mind when Darby lay dead in the road that night?" he asked.

"The same thing that went through my mind when Walter put that gun in his mouth and splattered his brains all over my bedroom wall," she paused, "relief."

Heath hugged her close. "Old Darby bit off more than he could chew when he decided to mess with my Maddie-cake, didn't he?"

"I guess he got more than he bargained for." Her breath was hot on his neck.

"He didn't know he was getting so much bang for his buck." He chuckled at his own joke. "I'm proud of you, Maddie."

"You might not be so proud of me when I tell you something else." She hesitated long enough that he pulled back to look at her.

"What is it?" His chest expanded with dread.

"There was a particular repercussion of the attack that I'm so ashamed of; my family doesn't even know—only Mark, and he's sworn to secrecy."

"Honey, you can tell me anything. I won't betray your confidence."

"I know you won't; that's why I'm telling you, but I'm kinda scared you'll be disappointed in me."

***

Maddie's tears left Heath's shirt wet, but she wasn't surprised by them. What did surprise her was him crying with her. Not a day passed in which she didn't struggle with her decision, and he understood because he knew her heart. He held her tight until they both drifted off to sleep.

When Maddie awoke, the temperature had dropped and her teeth chattered, but the weight of the world was no longer on her shoulders.

She shook Heath's arm. "Sweetie, let's take this party indoors. It's freakin' cold. I'm getting frostbite."

Taking his hand, she led him to the guest cottage where he promptly built a fire while she piled extra quilts on the bed. It was too cold to take their clothes off, so they cuddled up beneath the covers.

"This is probably the last cold snap," Heath said.

"I'm glad I got to spend it with you." Her teeth ached from containing her shivers.

He put his cold fingers under her chin and tipped it up until his lips brushed hers lightly.

"You're lucky it's so darn cold," Maddie said.

"Is that right? Were you planning to be the second woman to wrap her legs around me tonight?"

"Not a chance now that you reminded me. I don't want Carla's sloppy seconds."

Heath rolled on top of her. "I'd like to be your sloppy firsts…and seconds…and thirds." With every pause, he trailed kisses down her neck. "What do you say, Mad? Wanna get sloppy with me?"

With the cold forced out by the heat of their bodies, she struggled to think. A moan escaped her as he pushed her shirt up and his mouth followed.

He paused and lifted his head. "What do you want, Maddie?"

Her body ached with need and reflexively, she arched into him. "You."

"So, marry me, and you can have me anytime you want."

"This is blackmail." She writhed against him.

"All part of my plan." His hot breath scorched her skin.

"To withhold sex until I say yes?"

"That's Plan A." He nuzzled her neck.

"What's Plan B?"

"To get you knocked up, so you'll have to marry me?"

"I vote for Plan B. Let's practice." She reached for the button on his jeans.

He smiled against her neck. "Uh-huh, you little vixen. You're on the pill, aren't ya?"

"And I got checked for every STD under the sun after I found out about Mark."

He pressed up onto his elbows, letting cold air flood the space between them. "That's two libido killers in one statement." He rolled off of her and onto his back beside her.

Closing her eyes, she sighed. "I'm sorry."

He growled and pulled her on top of him. "I'm only kidding. As long as you marry me."

Maddie laughed. "You aren't going to give up, are you?"

"I'll have to resort to plan C."

"Which is what? Poke holes in the condoms and replace my pills with a placebo?"

"Hey, that's not a bad idea," he said. "But I was referring to patience. I don't want to wait to marry you, but I will. I won't stop asking though. I can't. You need to know every day how much I want you."

Freedom and acceptance filled her. "I won't get tired of hearing you say that. I love you, and one day when you ask, I'll be ready."

With the covers piled high and their clothes half on and half off, Maddie imagined she was a naughty teenager, squeezing in a quickie before curfew. The difference was that Heath took his time, and he knew what he was doing.

Chapter Twenty-two

Heath awoke to the sound of a door opening and the thump of kids' feet racing across the wood floors. Bracing himself, he shielded Maddie from the pounce, which was sure to follow.

"Mama, wake up. It's the rodeo today." Josh jumped on the bed.

"It's cold in here. Your fire's almost out," Jenny said, yanking the covers back and crawling under with them.

Frigid air tensed Heath's muscles until the heat cocooned them once again.

"Aunt Maddie, can I go to the rodeo too?" Nick asked, bouncing on the end of the bed.

Heath was glad he and Maddie had redressed after…

Lord, it was morning, and he was hard again. So inappropriate with the children in the bed. He burrowed into Maddie's side and willed his erection away.

He kissed Maddie's cheek. "I better go home and get Sara Ann, so we can get this show on the road-eo."

Maddie giggled. "We'll take my Suburban because I want my Nick-nock to come with us." Maddie sat up and gave Nick a noogie. "We'll come pick you guys up in a bit."

At home, Sara Ann wanted to wear her blue jeans with pink boots and a pink tutu.

Heath suppressed a smile. "I've never heard of a ballerina cowgirl." He shook his head. "You're one of a kind, sweet pea."

"I know, Daddy. Do I look pretty?" She twirled.

"You look beautiful, as usual." He took her little hand and rubbed his thumb across the back of it. "I think they're here, baby. Are you ready to go?"

She reached her arms up to him. "I don't think I want to ride a horse today, Daddy."

He scooped her up. "We're going to watch people ride horses and bulls. We don't get to do it ourselves. It'll be fun, you'll see."

He grabbed Sara Ann's booster seat and buckled her in the middle row with Jenny.

"We're gonna get cotton candy," Nick said from the third row. "What color do you want, Sara Ann?"

"Pink." She kicked her feet in excitement.

"Me and Josh are getting blue 'cause we're boys."

Heath could almost imagine Johnny, Nick's dad, saying something similar to him. Nick was known for repeating things his dad said, no matter how inappropriate.

Heath got behind the wheel. "We're outnumbered. How are we gonna keep up with four kids?"

Maddie cut her eyes and smirked at him. She leaned close to his ear before she spoke. "You know if we have a kid together, we'll have four kids. If that scares you, you may want to rethink whichever plan of yours included that option."

He tipped up one corner of his mouth. "I ain't scared." Taking her comment more like a challenge, he looked forward to the day she had his kid.

"Mr. Heath, how did you and my mama get to be such good friends?" Jenny asked.

Heath smiled at Maddie. "We were always friends, but we became good friends when my mama passed away."

"Did she go to heaven to live with Jesus and the angels?" Josh asked.

"Yeah, she did. One day they told me she had cancer, and three months later, we were having her funeral. It happened fast. She was very sick."

Maddie put her hand on his shoulder and squeezed.

He winked at her and continued, "Mama D made some food and brought it to our house. Maddie came, too. All the grownups were inside, and my big brother was in his room. I was sitting outside on the trampoline all alone when your mama found me.

"She rolled onto the trampoline and sat cross-legged next to me while she told me that her real dad went to heaven, but he wasn't sick like my mama. She also told me they're no sick people in heaven, so my mama was well." Heath didn't mention that Maddie had told him she'd seen his mom after her death. He'd wanted to ask her more about it, but had been too afraid.

"Then," Maddie said, "I asked him if he thought we could jump high enough to reach heaven and see my dad and his mom."

"We tried, didn't we, Maddie-cake?" He laced his fingers with hers. "The funny thing was Maddie was about as big as you are now Jenny. She was a tiny thing, and I wasn't. We tried holding hands and jumping at the same time—"

"But he kept messing up my bounce." Maddie grinned.

"So, eventually, your mama sat down, and I bounced her. She'd go really high, and her arms and legs would flail all over the place." He let go of her hand and threw his arm out to one side in imitation.

"Then, we switched and I tried to bounce you." Maddie laughed. "But that wasn't much fun for either of us, was it?"

"Did you see heaven?" Jenny asked.

"I didn't think so at the time. In fact, laughing with your mama kinda made me forget about it. But looking back, having Maddie there with me was like having a little piece of heaven on earth. It's still like that when I'm with her." He took her hand again.

Maddie smiled through her tears and kissed the back of his knuckles.

When they were almost to their destination,

Maddie laid down the ground rules. "Boys, do not run off without telling me or Mr. Heath where you're going and why. Stay together at all times. Got it?"

"Yes, ma'am," they said in unison.

"If I have to spend one moment panicked because I can't find you, guess what I'm gonna do?" Maddie asked.

"Tear our asses out of the frame?" Nick answered.

Heath coughed to cover his laugh, and Maddie ducked her head to hide her smile.

"Nick, don't cuss, baby." Maddie's words were choked. "You know better than to repeat things your daddy says."

"But I heard Big Daddy say that." His eyes went wide.

"Big Daddy's an adult so he can cuss if he wants to, but little kids can't." Maddie fought a smile.

"My papa cusses sometimes," Sara Ann said. "But he tells me I can't say the bad words."

"He's right, sweetheart," Maddie said. "Kids who cuss get their mouths washed out with soap."

"Yuck," Josh said.

Maddie looked at Heath. "When did this conversation get so off track?"

"The joys of parenthood. I wouldn't have it any other way." He aimed a slow wink at her.

Squeezing his hand, she bit her lower lip.

Damn, she was gorgeous.

At the rodeo, Heath carried Sara Ann while Jenny held Maddie's arm, and the boys ran ahead of them, chasing each other. They found seats on the metal bleachers just in time for Sara Ann to tell them she needed to go potty.

"I'll take her," Maddie said.

"Thanks. I'll keep an eye on the wild boys and Jenny-girl." Heath hugged Jenny to his side.

A few minutes passed before Jenny waved at someone. "Hey, Daddy."

Heath looked to see Mark and a blonde woman, making their way over to where they sat.

"Where's your mom?" Mark asked Jenny.

"Bathroom," Jenny said.

Mark frowned. "She left you here?"

"Mr. Heath is watching me and the wild boys."

"Oh." Mark looked at Heath. "Maddie wasn't sure you were coming. This is Christy."

Heath shook hands with the home wrecker and felt like he was betraying an unspoken code by being polite to the enemy.

"This is my first rodeo." Christy let out a throaty chuckle. "Does it always smell so bad at these things?"

"It's the aroma of nature." Heath and Jenny said it at the same time, and Jenny burst into giggles.

"Her grandfather, Big Dan, always says that," Mark explained to Christy.

The boys, who were seated on the row in front of Heath, were getting restless and rowdy, disturbing the people on either side.

"Fellas." Heath put a hand on each of their shoulders. "Settle down."

When he heard Sara Ann, Heath turned toward

her and met the squinty-eyed gaze of Mark. He supposed Mark didn't like another man disciplining his son, and he'd probably hear about it sooner or later. Twisting his lips, Heath wondered if Mark was man enough to say it to his face. Sometimes, it was good to be big and intimidating and in law enforcement.

"What are you doing here?" Maddie asked Mark.

"I wanted to be with my kids while they enjoy the rodeo."

The man knew the right thing to say, but Heath didn't believe him for a second.

"Mr. Heath," Nick said. "I gotta go pee."

"All right, Bud. Anyone else need to empty their bladder? Let's make one trip and be done with it." Heath stood.

"I could go," Josh said.

Mark stood, too. Looked like he would get his chance to bawl Heath out without Maddie hearing it.

Mark went into the john with the boys, while Heath waited outside. When Mark came back out, Heath was leaning against the cinder block building with his arms crossed over his chest.

"How's Maddie doing?" Mark asked.

Taken aback, Heath blinked. "Really good."

"She wasn't so good when I last saw her. Of course, she was probably still mad at herself about our intimate encounter when she spent the night with me, but she gets that way sometimes."

Heath deigned no reply. Mark was lying. Maddie wouldn't have sex with him.

"She's a spitfire in the sack. Red on the head, fire in the bed." Mark smirked.

A couple of knuckles cracked as Heath clenched his fist and resisted the urge to punch Mark in the face, but he was pretty sure Mark was provoking him on purpose. Violence would give him a good argument to keep his kids away from Heath.

"You shouldn't talk that way about the mother of your children. It's disrespectful." Heath opened his fingers to stretch his hands. "Besides, if she was so good, you wouldn't have screwed around on her."

"A man has certain fantasies and after what Maddie survived, I couldn't very well ask her to let me tie her up." Mark shrugged. "The others were for the kinky stuff."

"Others?" Heath tipped his head to one side. "So, there were more?"

Mark looked away and shoved his hands in the pockets of his khaki pants. After a moment's hesitation, he headed back to the bleachers.

Heath pushed open the bathroom door. "Boys, it doesn't take this long to pee."

Their laughter made him peek around the corner to see them having a water war in the sinks. He dried them off the best he could before he made his way back to the stands where his girls waited.

Chapter Twenty-three

It didn't take long for Maddie to grow tired of hearing Christy talk about how good Heath looked in his jeans. Mark looked pretty good naked, but he didn't hold the wick of a pillar candle next to Heath. Of course, Maddie didn't say any of that out loud. She'd definitely gotten the better end of that stick.

Heath sat next to her and pulled Sara Ann onto his lap. "What'd we miss?"

"You're just in time. Team roping is up next." Maddie nudged him with her shoulder.

Heath put his lips next to her ear. "I'd like to rope you later."

A shiver ran over her skin. The thought turned her on and terrified her at the same time. If there was anybody she trusted with rope, it was Heath. Even so, she still wasn't sure she could stand it.

Maddie glanced around and found Christy ogling Heath.

"I think you have a new fan," Maddie

whispered.

He cut his eyes to the side before he rolled them. "She can kiss it."

"I bet she'd do it with gusto." Maddie pressed her lips together.

Heath leaned closer. "To hear your ex talk, I'd say you're right."

Maddie's eyebrows climbed high. "Do tell. On second thought, I don't wanna know." She waved a hand.

"You're lucky to be rid of him, Mad. He doesn't seem to respect women very much, generally speaking."

Maddie almost asked, "Even me?" But she didn't really want to know that either. Before the divorce and before Heath, she'd thought Mark respected her. How could he not after he stayed by her side during her recovery? He'd put in the time and slowly gained her trust.

Now, she wondered if Mark had only seen her as a challenge. Maybe it had started that way, but she was sure he'd really loved her before it was over. Because she was guilty of it herself with the temporary insanity she'd had when she'd discovered he'd been unfaithful, she knew how loss and envy could make people act out of character sometimes. Mark behaved like a stranger more often than not these days.

She looked over at the man she'd shared so much of her life with and found him staring at her. Heath must have noticed because he snaked his arm around her back and rubbed circles with his palm.

"Well, look who's here." Carla Peterson's

voice produced the same physiological response as nails on chalkboard.

Maddie chuckled when Heath's tensed fingers dug into her back. If Carla tried to jump him again, Heath would use Maddie as a human shield.

Because she subsisted on Winston cigarettes and Mountain Dew, Carla was as skinny as a rail. Even so, her jeans were so tight they revealed a camel toe. Maybe she should smoke Camels, instead of Winstons. She'd also bought boobs at some point over the last ten or twelve years, and Maddie was sure that one of them would pop out of her low cut shirt at any moment.

"Is your boy competing today, Carla?" Maddie put on the doctor's wife expression she wore when forced to be polite to people she cared little about.

"Yeah, he's in the junior division. I'm surprised your kids aren't competing yet, Baker. Of course, not everyone can hack it. There's so much pressure, but then again, no one knows that better than you, seeing as how you gave it up."

"If Maddie had her way, they'd be out there," Mark said. "But as a physician, I'd rather not see my kids with broken necks."

"Oh, so you're the doctor Maddie couldn't hold on to?" Carla rested a hand on her bony hip.

The gloves were coming off. Maddie cleared her throat. "Tell me, Carla, did you leave Bart or did he leave you? Oh right, I remember now. He told me he caught his promiscuous wife riding the neighbor's horse bareback."

"He told me it was the delivery guy's horse," Heath said.

"It was probably both," Maddie and Heath said at the same time and laughed.

Carla narrowed her eyes. "You always thought you were so much better than everyone else, Maddie Baker. If your mama hadn't hit the jackpot and married for money, you'd be a poor, plain little thing like the rest of us."

Maddie rested assured, knowing Big Daddy had fallen quickly and madly in love with her mama. That love was still alive. They were the example for matrimony Maddie aspired to.

"No, she wouldn't," Mark said. "Maddie's got something you clearly don't. Class. She tried to take the high road, but you wouldn't allow it. Now, move on, you're blocking my kids' view."

After Carla stomped away, Christy had to put her two cents in. "Why are you defending your ex-wife? She has a new man who can stand up for her."

"Is that true, Maddie? Do you have a new man?" Mark asked. "Because you didn't mention it either of the two times we were in bed together during the last week."

"What?" Christy shrieked.

Sara Ann, who'd moved to sit in Jenny's lap in front of Mark, covered her ears and started to cry. "She hurt my ears, Daddy."

"Come here, baby." Heath took her from Jenny and stood. "It's okay, sweet pea. Are you happy now, Mark?"

Mark also stood. "No, I won't be happy until I get my wife back."

Christy rose, stomped her foot, and called Mark every name in the book until a burly, bearded security guard asked her to leave.

Heat flooded Maddie's face from all of the eyes glaring in their direction. It could be a new reality show. *Jilted: The Rodeo Edition.*

"Mama, are you getting back together with Daddy?" Jenny asked.

"No, baby." Maddie squeezed Jenny's shoulders. "Mark, you should go after Christy and see if you can fix it."

"I don't want her, Maddie. I'm in love with you."

"Can you people take your soap opera somewhere else? I'm here to see a rodeo, not an episode of Jerry Springer," a man behind them said.

Heath passed Sara Ann to Maddie. "Stay here." He turned to Mark. "Let's go."

Maddie tried not to smile as the blood drained from Mark's face before he followed Heath.

She turned to the man behind her. "Sorry about that."

"Ain't your fault, darlin'. You *was* trying to take the high road; I could tell. Bart's ex-wife is a real bitty. What'd you do to get on her bad side anyway?"

"We used to compete against each other in barrel racing and roping. She's a sore loser." Maddie tried to tamp down the smugness emanating from within.

"Hey, I remember you. You're Big Dan Baker's daughter. You and Bob Cook's boy were the Regional Champions in the nineties."

"Yes, sir." She nodded. "That was Heath who left a second ago."

"He's a hoss, ain't he?" The man looked off in the direction they'd gone.

"Yes, sir. I told him to get off the juice 'cause the horses are complaining." Maddie chuckled as the man did too. "I'm just teasing. He got those muscles the old-fashioned way, hard work."

And she loved every one of them.

***

Heath attempted to get Christy to patch things up with Mark out in the parking lot. His interference turned out not to be a good thing because Christy saw it as an invitation to grope him in front of Mark.

"Knock it off, Christy." Heath held her at arm's length. "Mark, you brought her. Take her and get the hell out of here."

"Don't get too comfortable with my wife because I'm going to find a way to get rid of you, muscle man." Mark opened his car door. "I hope your penis shrivels up and falls off."

"Thanks. It gives me the warm fuzzies knowing you're thinking about my third leg." Heath turned up one corner of his mouth.

"Get in the car, Christy," Mark said. "By the way, Heath, don't forget to ask Maddie about our time together in the blanket fort last weekend."

Heath stood, eyes narrowed, as they drove away. Determined *not* to ask Maddie about the fort, he told himself it didn't matter. He trusted her, and if anything had happened, she would've told him.

Doubt niggled at his mind. A lot had happened in the last week, including Maddie shooting and killing a rapist. The fort could have been the thing she'd wanted to talk to Heath about Sunday night.

When he returned to his seat, he sighed, realizing he hadn't seen much of the rodeo. There were too many distractions, and as soon as he sat down, the man behind them introduced himself and talked the rest of the day.

Later, when Heath buckled the kids into the car for the drive home, he was nearly as exhausted as they were. At least he didn't have dirt stuck to the cotton candy remnants on his face like they did. It was only because he hadn't eaten any.

"I'll drive," Maddie said. "You look beat."

"I can't let you do that."

"Yes, you can." She held out her hand for the keys. "I may be a woman, but I can drive."

He dangled them over her hand. "I seem to remember you running a certain Blazer into a ditch back in the day."

"Hey, we were muddin', and I'd had a little bit to drink." She grinned. "That was a fun night."

"A little bit?" He raised an eyebrow. "Yeah, the good ole days before cell phones." He shook his head and let go of the keys. "We lost our shoes walking knee deep in mud through Buddy Walker's field to call your dad to come get us out."

"It's a good thing Big Daddy loves you." Rising onto her tiptoes, she kissed his cheek.

When they were on the road with Maddie at the helm, she sighed. "I'm sorry about everything that happened today. I told Mark where we were going, but I never dreamed he'd show up. I'm not sure he's ever been to a rodeo."

"He wants you back bad, and he's looking for a

way to get me out of the picture." Heath's chest tightened, and he gripped the door handle.

"Heath, I hope you're not worried. First of all, if he wanted me so much, he should've kept his…" She glanced to the back seat, and so did he. The kids were dozing. "Yogurt-slinger in his own kitchen."

Heath laughed. "Maddie-cake, I love you." He leaned over to kiss her cheek. "Can I ask you something?"

"Anything."

He swallowed past a large lump in his throat. "What happened in the fort?"

"I'm not sure I want to say." She looked in the rearview mirror.

"Because of little ears?"

"That and you're going to be upset. Either with me or Mark, or maybe both of us." Her fingers tapped the wheel.

"So, what he said is true. You slept with him." Heath's voice sounded calm to his own ears, but his pulse pounded as heat spread up his neck.

"No. We didn't play hide the salami. Not even close." Her voice dropped to a whisper. "I'll tell you, but not with my kids in the car."

"It's okay. I don't wanna know." Heath turned to look out the window.

He did want to know, but he was an idiot for asking. Mark knew it would cause tension, and Heath had taken the bait after being above it all day.

"Heath-bar." Maddie reached to rub his thigh and grazed his groin. She jerked her hand away. "Sorry, that was an accident."

He checked the kids before adjusting himself. "Sure, it was. You're just like the rest of 'em. Can't keep your hands off me, can you?"

Maddie grimaced. "You're pretty irresistible. But if you think I like being grouped with a bunch of whores then you've got another thing coming. You're man enough to stop them from groping you, but don't because you like to have your ego stroked."

"Shit. Calm down. I was teasing you. It's like—"

"Like what, Heath?" Her red-haired temperament had her riled up.

"I don't want to argue with you, but it seems like you're trying to pick a fight with me."

The muscle in her jaw worked as she ground her teeth. She blew out a loud breath. "I'm sorry. I get that you were teasing me, but it was a little insulting." She ran her hand through her hair. "I am like the rest of them, aren't I?"

"Nope." He grinned. "I don't mind getting groped by the woman I love."

She chuckled, but he could tell she didn't mean it. She propped her elbow on the window and leaned her head into her free hand, away from him.

"You're tired, too. Pull over and let me drive." It was his turn to grope her thigh.

"Nah, I'm good." She straightened. "But I can't handle the late nights anymore. We're getting old. Just so you know…" She told him about Mark being at Southland and holding her while she'd cried herself to sleep.

The leather of the door handle groaned under

his fierce grip. That was Heath's job, not Mark's.

He needed to take preemptive measures against her ex, so he told Maddie about the phone call from Mark and the other things he'd said.

"I'm so sorry." She shook her head. "You must hate being caught in the middle of my drama. I'd understand if you wanted to cut me loose."

He put his hand on the back of her neck and rubbed her skin lightly. "Not a chance. You're mine, and I'm never letting you go. So, you might as well go ahead and marry me."

"Are you gonna marry Mr. Heath, Mama?" Jenny asked, leaning up from the back seat.

"Nice going," Maddie said out of the side of her mouth.

"Someday," Heath said to Jenny. "She's gonna marry me someday." He stroked Maddie's cheek with his thumb.

"Then Sara Ann will be my sister," Jenny said. "I've always wanted a little sister."

"You're only saying that because Josh quit letting you dress him up in your princess outfits." Maddie winked at her in the rearview mirror.

In under an hour, Maddie pulled up to Heath's house and got out to walk him and Sara Ann to the door.

"Can I see you later?" he asked.

"I might be able to sneak out in a little while. You want me to come over?"

"Can't wait. Text me when you leave." He hugged her, and with his kiss, he made her a promise.

A shudder ran through her. "I hope my dad

doesn't catch me. I might get grounded." Before she turned to go, she winked and blew him an air kiss.

He smacked her butt, and she swished it for him as she walked back to her car.

Damn. He shifted his feet, nonchalantly adjusting due to the tighter fit of his jeans.

Chapter Twenty-four

Maddie watched a movie with her family and couldn't wait for it to be over, so she could put her kids to bed and get to Heath's house. Imposing her own curfew, she intended to be back before midnight. Otherwise, she wouldn't get enough rest.

"You got a date, sugar?" her daddy asked. "You keep looking at the clock."

Everyone turned to her. Her response was to cross her eyes and stick out her tongue.

"Are you gonna spend the night with Mr. Heath again?" Jenny asked.

Her face probably turned as red as her hair. That wasn't the example she wanted to set for her kids, so she furrowed her brow and shook her head. It wasn't an outright lie.

Grabbing a plastic bowl with nothing but popcorn kernels in the bottom, she followed her mom into the kitchen. "What am I gonna do, Mama?"

"You better marry that boy before your kids figure out you're living in sin."

"Mama." Maddie's voice was a loud whisper before she glanced over her shoulder. "We aren't…living in sin…exactly." Her gaze landed on her feet.

"Really? Well, what are you waiting for?" Her mama tilted her head to one side. "Get you some, girl."

"Mama!"

"Don't give me that prudish ice princess business. You're a grown woman with needs. Heath seems equipped to meet them." Mama D's expression softened. "And you're in love with each other."

"In that case, I'm going over there, and I might stay all night." Maddie put her hands on her hips.

Her mama smirked. "Good for you."

"Hold on." Big Daddy approached them. "Where do you think you're going, young lady? If you're thinking about sneaking out, I'd like to remind you about the time Heath brought you home about sunrise, and I was waiting with the shotgun." Humor laced his voice.

Maddie put her hands up. "Now, Daddy, you know we weren't like that back then."

"But you are now? I'm gonna talk to that boy. Give him a pat on the back." Big Daddy winked at her as he slid his arms around her mama's waist. "You're still my baby girl. You know that, don't cha?"

"Yes, sir." She hugged them both and made a funny face at the man who'd adopted her as a young girl. He loved her and her sisters like they were his own blood, and he loved their mama with all his heart. Family was their life.

Mama D giggled at being caught in the middle of the group hug. Or maybe Big Daddy was doing something perverted to her. They still acted like teenagers sometimes, making Maddie wonder again what they'd been doing when Big Daddy had his heart attack.

She let them go and stepped back.

"We'll put the kids to bed if you want to head out." Her dad grinned. "Try not to stay up all night though. You get a little fractious when you don't get enough sleep, sugar."

She laughed and sighed at the same time. "All right, Daddy."

It was beyond weird for her parents to encourage her to go spend the night with a man who wasn't her husband. They clearly loved Heath a whole bunch. She sure did, but the growing intensity and dependency of it scared her a little. If their relationship fell apart, she would be crushed again.

She hesitated at the door of her truck. If she was going to do this, she needed to commit. Why was she always trying to talk herself out of it? The logical reasons were all there, but they conflicted with what was in her heart. Should she follow it? Should she go all in?

At the end of the driveway, she stopped to text Heath before leaving Southland. She also checked under her seat to be sure her rape whistle was there before she put her car back in drive.

Heath didn't reply to her text, so when she arrived at his house, she knocked lightly on the front door. When he didn't answer, she tried the handle. It was unlocked.

She walked down the hallway to his empty room. After depositing her bag on the bed, she went to the door with the pink pony hanging on it. There he was asleep in Sara Ann's bed. The little cutie was awake beside him, and she waved at Maddie.

Carefully, she slid out of the bed, not disturbing her daddy. She took Maddie's hand and pulled her down the hallway to the kitchen.

In a quiet voice, Sara Ann said, "I was waiting for you to come." She wrapped her arms around Maddie's legs. "I love you, Miss Maddie. Jenny's so lucky to have a mama."

Maddie picked her up and hugged her close. "I love you too, baby. Your daddy, too."

"If you wanted to live here, you could. We have enough rooms for Jenny and Josh and even Nick, if I let him have my playroom."

Maddie smiled. "That's so sweet of you to offer your playroom. But Nick's my nephew, not my son, so he has to live with his mom and dad."

"Do you want to see a picture of my mama, the real one who moved to heaven?" Her little eyebrows were raised.

"Show me." Maddie put Sara Ann down, and she ran to the bookshelf next to the entertainment center.

Sara Ann pulled out a photo album and climbed onto the couch. She patted the seat next to her and Maddie took it, putting an arm around the sweet girl and pulling her close to her side.

Sara Ann opened the cover and turned pages, one at a time. Maddie stopped her to point out a class picture from the fourth grade.

"Look who it is," Maddie said.

"Who?" Sara Ann furrowed her brow.

"That little red-haired girl is me…and that little dark haired boy behind me is your daddy."

"Ooh." She sang as she studied the picture and then looked back and forth to Maddie's face. "My hair's brown like my daddy's."

"Yeah, it is. And it's beautiful, just like you." Maddie tweaked her nose and then twirled her hair.

Sara Ann turned the page and pointed to a wedding picture of Glenn and Anna. "That's her."

"Wow, she was really beautiful, wasn't she?" Maddie's heart half broke for the little girl who would only know her parents from photographs. Maddie could mostly relate.

Sara Ann smiled a proud smile and nodded her head. "I think I miss her."

The hair stood up on the back of Maddie's neck, and she clenched her jaw and closed her eyes. "I was young when my real daddy died, too. I have a picture of him that I look at sometimes, but my older sisters remember him better than I do. It used to make me sad, but you know what?"

"What?" Sara Ann looked up at her.

"After my dad went to heaven, I got another one who took really good care of me. It's kind of like your daddy. He takes really good care of you, doesn't he?"

"Yes, ma'am, but I didn't get a mama yet."

Sara Ann sat silent for a moment. "You could be my mama if you want to."

Maddie had walked right into that one. "That'd be the best job in the whole world." She squeezed Sara Ann closer. "Things have a way of working out when they're supposed to. We'll know when the time is right."

Sara Ann leaned against Maddie's side and turned another page. "That's my papa with a mustache." She giggled. "It looks funny."

"I remember when he had that. My daddy did, too. They used to grow out their beards during hunting season and then leave a mustache until summer came."

"How come?" Sara Ann glanced up.

"They said the beards kept them warm when it was cold outside. The mustaches were just to be funny, I guess." Maddie shrugged.

"How come girls don't grow beards?"

"Cause we don't want anything to cover up your pretty face," Heath said from the entrance to the hall.

He was leaning against the wall, and Maddie suspected he'd been there for a while, listening and watching. Heat curled low in her belly at the sight of him. In his bare feet with rumpled hair, a white T-shirt straining across his shoulders, and low slung jeans, he had to be the sexiest man alive.

"Hey, handsome," Maddie said.

"Daddy, I showed her the pictures. Look, here you are when you were little. And Miss Maddie, too." Sara Ann flipped through the book.

Heath came over, picked Sara Ann up, and sat

back down with her in his lap. Maddie's heart turned somersaults. He waited patiently while Sara Ann turned the pages and pointed to pictures. Maddie imagined this was a little ritual they performed often, so she rested her chin on his shoulder and observed.

Heath readjusted to put his arm around Maddie, too. Leaning into his warmth, her eyes grew heavy.

***

Heaven on earth was what Heath had in his arms. Between Sara Ann and Maddie, he thought his chest might burst open. He needed to figure out a way to get Maddie to say yes to his proposal.

He was seriously considering flushing her birth control pills when a thought occurred to him.

The ring. His mother's ring, the same one Anna wore when she'd married Glenn, was nestled in its velvet case in his sock drawer.

Mark had probably given her a boulder-sized diamond, and his mama's ring wouldn't touch it in an appraisal. But it would be perfect for Maddie because she'd appreciate the sentimental value.

Sara Ann yawned and rubbed her eyes. He'd be able to put her in bed soon.

He leaned forward to peer at Maddie and found her asleep. They were out of sync at times, and the thought made him remember her earlier words about how they'd know when it was right. He kissed the top of Maddie's head, hoping it would be soon.

When he got up to take Sara Ann to bed, Maddie awoke and flashed him a sleepy smile. Instead of following him, she stretched out on the couch and closed her eyes.

Knowing how exhausted she must be, he hated to wake her. He squatted next to the couch and brushed her hair back. "Come sleep in my bed."

She groaned and yawned. "Carry me."

He scooped her up and took her to his room. She chuckled as he put her down. Leaving her by the bed, he went to close and lock the door, just in case.

When he turned back, she held two relatively short lengths of nylon rope in her hands, and his eyebrows hit his hairline. Based on her experience, this would be very hard for her. He saw it as a chance to right a wrong, not that he could erase what happened, but he would use every ounce of love he had to help heal her.

Breathing slowly to calm his racing heart, he pulled his T-shirt over his head. "Me first."

"I've never done anything like this before, Heath." Her voice was shaky.

He leaned in and nuzzled her neck, right next to her ear. "You'll figure it out. You know how to work that rope, so I'm going to lay back and let you have your way with me."

She bit her lip as she made a loose artillery loop and slipped it around his right wrist. It was the knot he'd planned to use on her because it was easy to get out of if she panicked. She secured his other wrist before she crawled onto the bed.

"I kinda like this." She smiled as she straddled his waist. "It shows off all of your muscles." She ran her fingertips lightly across his chest and down his arms until she was leaning close to his face.

Chills raced along his skin even as blood rushed through his veins like wildfire.

"I appreciate your efforts to look so good." She sat up and looked him in the eyes. "You're gorgeous."

Involuntarily, he twitched and her eyebrows shot up.

"Oh, I think someone likes hearing how gorgeous they are," she practically sang the words.

"I like hearing that you appreciate it." He twitched again, this time on purpose.

She started kissing his earlobe and didn't stop until she'd done a thorough job covering a lot of ground. Nearly all his ground. His grip on the bindings had completely relaxed, as had his entire being.

She crawled up his body until her face was close to his, a sexy smirk on her lips. "You were holding on for dear life, cowboy."

"A trick I learned from saddle bronc competition. Hold on, find the rhythm, and enjoy the ride." He winked.

Her smile bloomed, and he pulled free of the ropes, sitting up as he wrapped his arms around her. Taking the hem of her shirt, he pulled it over her head. He rolled them over, and she trembled.

"Shh, Maddie. Look at me. Only if you ask me to, okay?"

She nodded and put her hands in his hair to pull his face down to hers. He was naked, but she wasn't, so he spent the next few moments getting her that way.

After he removed her lacy underwear, she took

a deep breath. "Okay. I'm ready."

"Ready for what?" He had to be sure.

"For you to tie me up." She spread her arms out to the sides.

"Any time you need to pull free, just do it." His lips brushed hers. "We have the rest of our lives to play."

Her shy smile hit him in the gut a second before she nodded. He fixed the loose knot around one wrist and kissed his way down her arm. With a light touch of his lips, he blazed a trail across her chest and up her other arm to the wrist where he looped the rope around it. She lay perfectly still, in all her beauty, watching him with cautious optimism.

He wanted to take away every bad memory. But since that wasn't possible, he intended to replace them with mind-blowingly wonderful ones.

Propping on his elbow next to her, he gently pulled a section of her long locks and let it slip lightly through his fingers. "Maddie, your hair is like spun silk.

"Your eyes are the color of a clear sky on a hot summer's day." He kissed one eyelid then the other.

He ran his thumb lightly across her lips. "Your lips are like the softest rose petal." He tasted them with the same delicacy he would if he were touching an actual flower.

Next, he ran his fingers along her jaw, down her throat, and across her collarbone. "Your skin is like porcelain."

Continuing in this manner, he covered nearly every inch of her beautiful body before he returned to her mouth. It held a happy smile, which creased the corners of her eyes. A flare of victory ignited in his core. She hadn't pulled free.

"I love you so much, Heath," she said. "The only bad thing about this is I want to wrap my arms around you so much it's killing me."

"Well, you ain't dying on my watch." He tugged her wrists, and the ropes fell away.

In an instant, her arms encircled him. As his lips covered hers, he wrapped her tighter in his embrace. He had her love and trust, but he didn't want to wait a second longer to have her hand.

Chapter Twenty-five

At daybreak, Maddie opened her eyes. With Heath's warm body spooning her from behind, she smiled at the cut end of braided rope in her line of sight. A bubble of pride swelled in her core. She'd done something she never thought she'd be able to do.

It wasn't just the feeling of accomplishment washing over her, it was the belief that something broken inside her was right again. With his soft lips, tender touch, loving eyes, and life-giving words, Heath had mended the gash in her mind where the ugliness had resided. She couldn't promise it would never try to rear up again, but she had so much good to drown the bad the battle would be easier.

Lifting both hands to adjust her pillow, she fully intended to snuggle in for a few more minutes, even though she needed to get home. Blinking, she wondered briefly if she was dreaming. The metal on her left ring finger felt real as she pressed it with the tip of her thumb.

Sitting up in bed to get a better look in the pale light, the familiar design sparked a warm glow in the center of her chest. The Claddagh had belonged to Heath's mama. In Maddie's vague memories, Mrs. Cook had been a sweetheart who was proud of her Irish heritage. She'd once teased Maddie about them being related because of their red hair.

"Don't freak out." Heath sat up next to her. "I tried it on your finger to see if it needed to be resized, and you closed your fist, so I couldn't get it off."

"Likely story." She cocked an eyebrow before her lips tipped up at the corners, and she examined her hand again, flaring her fingers. "It's a perfect fit."

"I know." He kissed her shoulder. "You don't have to take it off, but I understand that you might not be ready for your family to see you wearing my ring just yet."

"I can wear it whenever I sneak out to come see you." She wriggled her eyebrows. "Just until I'm ready to go public, okay?"

"So, we're secret lovers then?" His lips found the sweet spot behind her ear. "Hmm, that's kind of sexy."

Maddie moaned as her body reacted to his touch, forcing her thoughts into the background.

What was I going to say? Oh, yeah.

Brushing the backs of her knuckles across his stubble-covered jaw, she met his hot gaze, and nearly lost her train of thought again. "I'm glad you're not upset with me. I need you to know I'm not embarrassed of you, but Jenny asked me if I was spending the night with you again in front of my parents, and it freaked me out. I don't know how to explain this to my kids. It feels right, and it feels wrong at the same time."

He tucked a loose strand of hair behind her ear. "Maddie, try not to overthink it. Your kids want to see you happy. I know you're struggling with making the right decisions, but don't forget I'm right here with you."

"How could I? Mr. Unforgettable." Her hands cupped his face as she leaned closer for a kiss.

Ten minutes and two orgasms later, Maddie buttoned her jeans and put her boots on.

"I'm really happy right now." Heath rolled out of bed and put on pajama bottoms. "But I'll be especially happy on the day when you don't have to leave me."

Maddie admired him while she pulled her hair into a ponytail. She considered herself damn lucky to be the recipient of all the lovin' Heath had to offer. Every part of her tingled with satisfaction.

He walked her to her car and kissed her goodbye. "We'll be over a little later."

Maddie drove home with a contented grin on her face, until she looked at the steering wheel and noticed her hand. Her eyes bulged. The gold glinted in the early morning sun. If she remembered the Claddagh positions correctly, having it situated on her left ring finger with the bottom of the heart toward her fingertips indicated she was an engaged woman.

She couldn't deny what she wanted. Heck, she

wanted to be married to Heath pronto, not only because she enjoyed the married things they did together, in the sack and out of it, but because she was totally and completely in love with the man. There would be no better way to spend the rest of her life than by his side as his wife and partner.

Should she? Was it too soon to move on with her life? Wavering thoughts jockeyed for top place in her mind.

When she pulled in the gate at Southland, she let out a long breath, and her concerns escaped with it. Life needed to be lived. It might try to buck her, but she planned to hold on for the ride.

Her mama was the first person to notice the ring. "Does this mean what I think it means?"

Maddie twisted her lips, but couldn't conceal her shit-eating grin.

Squealing, her mama hugged her tight and rocked them side to side.

"Don't make a big deal out of it yet, Mama." Maddie squelched her own enthusiasm. "I need to talk to the kids."

After breakfast, Maddie took her kids out to saddle their horses before Heath and the rest of the family joined them.

Pondering how to approach the subject, she finally just blurted it out. "What would you guys think if I married Mr. Heath?"

"Yay!" Josh shouted and jumped up, spooking his horse.

"Whoa, Santana." Maddie placed the flat of her hand on the gelding's neck, instantly calming him. Sometimes, she believed she'd inherited a gift for working with animals from her mama and grandfather.

"Sorry," Josh said. "Mr. Heath's so cool, and he's got big muscles like The Rock. Will he be my new dad?"

"He'll be our step-dad, Josh," Jenny said. "I think you should go for it, Mama. Mr. Heath's really sweet, and he makes you smile."

"Will Sara Ann be our sister?" Josh asked. "'Cause I need a brother too."

Maddie laughed. "You've got your cousin Nick, who's your best bud and like a brother."

"I know, but if you and Mr. Heath make a baby, I'm requesting a boy so the numbers will be equal. 'Kay?" Josh's brow wrinkled between his eyes, showing he was dead serious.

Maddie cleared her throat. "We don't get to decide what the sex of the baby will be. That's up to God." *If there's a baby. Lord, help me.*

"Well, I'll start praying about it." Josh turned back to his mount. "I prayed for God to send you a new husband, and Mr. Heath showed up. So I know he listens to me."

"In that case, pray that God will wait a year or two before he blesses us with that brother of yours." Maddie winked.

"Okay," Josh said. "We'll name him Glenn."

Maddie jerked her head around, but Josh had moved on, checking the stirrups and getting ready to ride. She wondered if her son had overheard them mention Heath's deceased brother, or if her child had inherited some of the supernatural juju which seemed to run in their family. A chill raced over her skin.

"Mama, can I ride your old stud Leroy?" Jenny asked.

Maddie inhaled sharply and promptly choked on the saliva flooding her windpipe. "Wha-What?"

"You know? Leroy." Jenny cut her eyes. "Uncle Johnny said you used to call him *your old stud* before they gelded him."

A chuckle gurgled in Maddie's chest. "Baby, Leroy's old, and I only ride him once in a while. Back in the day, he was the fastest thing on four legs, so I'm nervous about you riding him."

"But I want to try barrel racing, Mama." She poked her bottom lip out so far she could've tripped over it.

"You hop on Daisy and go ride with your brother. I'll see if I can round up Leroy."

Jenny's pout exploded into a grin. "Big Daddy said he was probably in the front pasture."

Maddie knew that's where Leroy was because she'd slowed to see him on her way home that morning. Grabbing his halter and a lead line to hook on her saddle next to her catch rope, she mounted Rosco.

Moments later, Maddie walked across the open pasture where several of God's creatures eyed her with suspicion. The donkey kicked at nothing, and the goat fainted. Maddie contained her laugh, shook her head, swung her rope and missed.

Heath's truck on the driveway had distracted her. She actually didn't need the lariat because Leroy walked right to her and nickered. She put the halter on her *old stud*. Hearing those words come from the mouth of her eight-year-old had been a bit of a shock. Maddie had referred to Leroy that way fifteen years before Big and Rich had made it famous in their song "Save a Horse, Ride a Cowboy".

Heath parked his truck by the fence and leaned on the top rail, so she got back on Rosco and led Leroy over to where Heath waited.

He propped his arms on the fence. "Do you have any idea how incredibly glorious you look on horseback?"

The memory of another kind of ride caused a little heat to creep into her cheeks.

The back window of the truck rolled halfway down. "Hey, Miss Maddie. You look like the people at the rodeo."

"Thank you, baby." Maddie winked. "Y'all get on up to the barn. I'll meet you there in a few minutes."

"I can't tear my eyes away," Heath said.

"Stop it. You're making me blush."

"That looks good on you, too."

Maddie shifted the reins left to turn Rosco. "See you up there."

She clicked her tongue and gave Leroy's lead a slight tug.

***

A small flash of gold reflecting the sun caught Heath's attention as Maddie turned away. His smile broadened. He hoped it meant she was ready to go public.

"Yeehaw," he yelled as he jumped back into his truck.

Sara Ann's sweet voice filled the air as she sang, "Yeeeehaaaaaaaaaw."

They found Johnny in the barn, saddling horses.

"Hey, Sara Ann," Nick said. "You can ride with me on Bo Duke. My dad is riding Luke."

"Yeehaw," she said.

"Yeehaw," Nick responded.

Johnny helped Nick into the saddle and then lifted Sara Ann up to join him. "The word of the day is *Yeehaw*. Especially, for you, brother. Welcome to the family."

Johnny extended his hand, and when Heath clasped it, Johnny pulled him into a hug.

After a quick pat on the back, Heath stepped back, unable to hide his smile. "What did Maddie tell you guys?"

Johnny shrugged with a grin. "Nothing specific, but she's sporting a new piece of jewelry. It's a little symbolic."

"It's an old piece of jewelry actually," Heath said. "It's been in my mom's family for at least five generations."

"That's really something," Johnny said.

"Maddie's worth it." The ring meant a lot to Heath, but having Maddie's love was everything.

"Speak of the she-devil," Johnny said as Maddie brought Leroy into the barn.

"Hey, that's my future wife you're talking about." Heath bowed up.

Maddie smiled as she passed Johnny the lead rope and wrapped her arms around Heath's neck. He placed his hands around her waist and pulled her in for a smooch.

"You smell like Leroy," he said when he broke the kiss.

"But you love me anyway."

"Damn right, I do." He smacked her on the butt.

Once Big Dan joined them, they headed out on the Southland property. Johnny and the kids rode ahead, followed by Heath, Maddie, and Big Dan, riding three abreast.

"I need help planning a big event." Heath chuckled as Maddie's eyes grew wide. "A birthday party for a four-year-old girl."

"Pony rides would be fun for the kids," Big Dan said. "I know a guy."

"Can you find out how much he charges?" Heath asked as his butt itched in the vicinity of his thin wallet. The Bakers didn't have that issue. "I've budgeted for a few things, but there's this stupid trend where the kid having the birthday gives goody bags to the guests. It's ridiculous, but Sara Ann gets them at every party we go to, and she's already talking about what she wants to put in her bags."

"I can help with that," Maddie said. "We can catalog order in bulk to cut costs."

"And," Big Dan said, "if he's not already booked, my buddy won't charge me a thing. He owes me a favor."

Tension slid off Heath's shoulders. "That would be a huge help. Thank you."

"Heath, you've always been like family," Dan said. "I'm glad you made Maddie see sense and keep that ring on her finger. How long do you think we'll have to wait before the big day?"

Maddie gasped. "Daddy."

"Dan, I'm trying very hard not pressure her. If it were up to me, I'd tie the knot today." His face warmed as he thought of the knots and rope from the night before. "But Maddie needs more time. I'll let her name the date when she's ready."

"Smart man." Dan nodded.

"Thank you," Maddie said to Heath. "I'm gonna turn Leroy loose and see what he's got before I let Jenny ride him." She nudged her horse, and they took off, leaving a cloud of dust in their wake.

"Danny and Liz will be here in about a month. It sure would be a nice surprise to have a wedding while they're here," Dan said.

"I don't know about that." Heath shook his head, a little niggle of unease clogging his throat. "Maddie will think it's too soon."

"Leave it to us." Dan's eyes glinted with mischief. "We'll see what we can work out. Do you want a big wedding? Because I'll go on and tell you Maddie had a big one the first go-round, against her will. She put on a happy face, but Dixie and Mark's mom went overboard."

"I can't imagine Maddie liking that very much." Heath thought for a moment. "I picture Maddie and me with our kids, you guys, and my dad."

"You can do it here at Southland. Heck," Dan gestured to his horse, "you could do it on horseback. That'd be perfect for you two."

Heath's vision expanded to include the two of them in white shirts and cowboy hats.

196

Chapter Twenty-six

The following week, Maddie chewed a couple of Tums before she drove the kids to Atlanta for their weekend with Mark. Her news would not be well received.

Following the kids to the door, she took a deep breath. Mark hugged Jenny then Josh. Once they were inside, he held the door and gazed at Maddie. She squirmed. It wasn't his lustful look. His expression held a promise. The one he'd made to her on their wedding day that he would always love her and always be there for her.

"Come in." His voice was soft and inviting.

Entering the kitchen, she took a seat at the round breakfast table, where their foursome used to share informal meals.

The kids went to their rooms, and Mark poured them each a glass of sweet tea. He sat next to her and bumped her glass with his, just like old times.

Before she got distracted with a trip down

memory lane, she fisted her hands. "Jenny wants to try competitive barrel racing."

Mark furrowed his brow, but kept silent for a long moment. "I suppose we could get her lessons."

A small smile tipped the corners of Maddie's mouth as relief rounded her shoulders. "I've worked with her a little. She's ridden Leroy, and she's a natural, Mark. It blew my mind."

"I feel better with you teaching her anyway." He smiled and slid his hand across the table, gripping Maddie's. "Christy moved out."

It was Maddie's turn to crinkle her brow.

"I told her she had to go. I made a huge mistake, Maddie. I love you. I want you back, darlin'."

Maddie opened her mouth to speak, but he cut her off. "I know it'll be hard to forgive me, but I want to see a marriage counselor and work things out."

"I'm marrying Heath," she blurted.

His forehead creased before he smoothed it and tipped up one corner of his mouth. "You can't do that, darlin'. He's just a rebound. You were so devastated over what happened between us that you sought comfort in his arms." His tone took on that of an authority figure speaking to a small child. "I understand and I forgive you."

Her entire body tensed, and she pasted a false smile on her face and spoke through clenched teeth. "Heath's not my rebound guy. You were, all those years ago, when we met. Sure, I was getting over something traumatic, but I wanted Heath and I thought he'd rejected me. I clung to you because he was no longer available." Her expression softened as she sighed. "I'm sorry, and I'm not sorry at the same time."

He'd let go of her hand as she spoke, and he fidgeted. "How can you be so cruel, Maddie? We shared twelve years together, two of them healing you and ten of them married and having a beautiful family. You can't lie to me or yourself and say it meant nothing, that you didn't love me."

"I didn't say that. I did love you, Mark. Part of me always will. My life with you meant everything to me, but it wasn't everything I wanted or dreamed of for myself." She winced inside. Her honesty sounded harsh even to her, and she didn't want to be a heartless bitch.

He tilted his head. "What do you mean?"

Briefly, she closed her eyes. Opening them, she met his gaze. "I want the country, not the city. I want boots and blue jeans, not heels and slacks. I like wearing cutoffs in the summertime over my bathing suit, but that embarrasses you. There are a lot of things I gave up about myself to please you." She turned a palm up then dropped it. "Don't get me wrong. I know every relationship has compromises, but with Heath, I get to be myself. He loves me, warts and all."

"You have warts?" His eyebrows shot up.

Maddie laughed at the panic stricken look on his face. "No, not unless there's something you need to tell me."

He let out a noise of exasperation. "Maddie, please don't marry him yet. Give me another chance." Tears welled up in his eyes, and he got on his knees in front of her and clutched her hands. He let go when he saw the ring on her finger.

"Maddie, no." He covered his face with his palms and sat back on his heels.

His reaction tugged at her heartstrings, and she reached out to him. Mark laid his head on her chest, and she squirmed at the intimacy of their position.

He pulled back and looked at her. "I'm going to be a better man, Maddie. You can be yourself with me. I'm going to be the husband you need and the father our kids deserve."

Maddie couldn't believe he was still at it. "Speaking of our kids, come out to Southland and watch Jenny practice sometime. Your support would mean so much to her."

"I'll be glad to. I'm so happy you're willing to work with me, Maddie." He hugged her and nuzzled her boobs with his head.

She pushed him away. "Don't misunderstand, Mark. I'm willing to work with you to parent our kids, but as for our marriage, it's over. Heath is my future, and you need to accept it and find a way to get along with him."

Chapter Twenty-seven

The day of the birthday party arrived, and Heath gave Maddie a big kiss when she arrived early to help him and his dad decorate. The Bakers had gone to a lot of trouble for them, and Sara Ann was thrilled to have such a big tadoo for her special day.

Johnny brought a helium tank and was blowing up a hundred pink and blue balloons. Sara Ann only wanted pink, but Josh reminded her that he and Nick would be at the party, and boys liked blue.

When Dan arrived with his horse trailer, Sara Ann begged to go see the pony, while she did a combination skip-jump maneuver Heath referred to as the dance stomp. He thought with the dance lessons she'd taken she should look more graceful, but that was how she displayed her excitement and he loved it. She'd also done it when Maddie had told her she was going to marry him and be her new mama.

Heath picked Sara Ann up and carried her over to watch Dan unload the pony and put him in the corral. She wouldn't stay still in his arms, so he put her down. She performed the dance stomp on Heath's toes.

Thank God for boots.

"What do you think, pretty girl?" Big Dan asked her. "His name is Star because of this pattern on his nose."

"I have a play horse named Star, too," Sara Ann said.

"I rode him already to make sure he's safe for kids," Josh said. "You can pet him, Sara Ann."

Josh stood on one side of the horse, and Nick was on the other, holding the lead line. Sara Ann stepped closer, rubbed the horse then ran back to hug Heath's legs and put some more dust on his boots. After repeating the process several times, she started loving on the pony more than her daddy.

"You like Star, don't cha, baby girl?" Heath's dad asked after joining them.

Her proud smile lit up her beautiful little face. "Yeah, Papa. I'm gonna ride him all by myself."

"Ooh, can I hold the lead?" Papa asked.

"Yeah." She stomped around some more.

Heath smiled, knowing she would sleep very hard that night, which meant he and Maddie could make as much noise as they wanted in their private rodeo.

Big Dan, whom Sara Ann now called Big Daddy like the other kids, put her in the saddle and her papa led her around the corral. She was riding all by herself as Maddie snapped pictures.

With a heart bursting at the seams, Heath snaked his arms around her waist from behind. She lowered the camera and leaned against him.

"I'm not sure I've ever seen her so happy. Thank you, Maddie-cake." He kissed her neck.

Big Dan strolled over. "I don't want to hear any objections from you, Heath, but I'm giving Star to Sara Ann as a birthday present."

Heath grazed Maddie's shoulder as he took a step back and clutched a hand over his heart. "No, Dan. We can't accept it. It's too much."

"Your dad's springing for the tack, so it's a joint venture. Plus, my other young grandkids might enjoy riding the pony when they get a little older. Sara Ann makes eleven. I need two more to make it a Baker's dozen. Get to work, son."

Heath widened his eyes and spoke out of the corner of his mouth. "We're not married yet."

"Uh-huh." Dan dipped his chin and shifted his eyes to one side.

"Daddy, cut it out." Maddie slapped Dan's arm. "We already have three kids, so we can wait a little while to add to the brood."

"I'm glad you're adopting Sara Ann, sugar." Dan hugged Maddie. "Adopting you and your sisters was one of the best moves I ever made. I love you as if I'd spawned you myself."

She looked up at him. "I know, Daddy. I love you too, as if you were my natural father. Thank you for the pony for Sara Ann."

Heat radiated from the center of Heath's chest right down to his toes. With her words, Maddie claimed Sara Ann as hers. A loving mother was what he'd always wanted for his daughter. And Maddie was *who* he always wanted for himself.

***

Later that night, Maddie closed Heath's bedroom door. "You owe me big time for today."

His lips landed on her neck and kissed a path down to her collarbone. "Why do you say that?"

"All of the single moms were giving me the evil eye…for taking you off the market. Ahh…" The gasp came when his mouth found one of her sensitive spots.

"I'll make it up to you, beautiful," he said around a mouthful of skin.

All other thoughts dissolved as she came apart in his arms. Afterward, she remembered what else she'd wanted to tell him.

"Danny, Jane, and Liz are coming to town next week. They want to go rafting down the Ocoee— adults only. You interested?" She stroked his chest with her fingertips.

"Sounds fun. I'll try to work it out so Sara Ann can stay with my dad."

"If he's busy, Mama D and Big Daddy are keeping all the kids for the day. You know how thrilled they are to have her in the family…and you too."

"Show me. I want to know how thrilled they are." His husky voice sent chills along her skin.

Hot damn. "Okay, cowboy, but I may have to strap you down for this. I'm not sure you can handle it."

Maddie couldn't believe the things that came out of her mouth in her private moments with

Heath. She'd never really been herself with Mark. Of course, she'd been trying to figure out who she was early in their relationship, and she'd never been completely satisfied with who she'd settled for.

Heath had freed her from the little box she'd put herself in. He'd taught her she didn't have to compartmentalize her life. She could be a mother, a lover, and every other role she needed to fill and still be happy and in control of her own decisions. With Heath by her side, she could tame wild stallions.

Heath was begging for mercy before she finished with him. Then he returned the favor.

There was a light knock on the door. "Daddy, I heard a noise."

Maddie slipped on a robe while Heath put on pajama pants and opened the door to Sara Ann.

"Hey, sweet pea." He bent and picked her up. "What noise did you hear?"

"I think Star was hollering 'cause he's scared of being in a new place." She rubbed her eyes.

Fire burned in Maddie's cheeks, and she put her hand over her mouth. She'd been the one hollering. Heath had told her she could.

"You want to go outside and check on Star?" he asked.

"Yes, sir." She nodded.

Maddie and Heath got dressed and grabbed flashlights for the walk through the woods to the stables. Maddie was at home in the woods at Southland, but these spooked her a little. The hair on the back of her neck stood up.

Vague recollections of seeing spirits when she

was young flitted through her mind. They were thoughts she'd buried deep and didn't visit often. She'd seen Big Daddy's first wife at Southland and Heath's mom at his house, but she'd turned it off so long ago, she questioned if it had ever been real.

Although she didn't see them, Maddie suspected Glenn and Anna's spirits were nearby, watching over Sara Ann.

A shiver ran down her spine. She latched on to Heath's free arm, and he moved to wrap it around her.

In the stable, they checked on Star and found him safe and sleepy. Sara Ann smiled, clearly feeling better knowing her new pet was comfortable.

Back at the house, they put Sara Ann in her bed, and when Heath closed the door to his room, he grinned. "Okay, maybe not so loud this time, cowgirl."

Chapter Twenty-eight

Maddie stuck her hand out to stop Josh. "Give Mama a kiss."

A sticky peck landed on her cheek before he dashed after Nick.

Jenny ran to Maddie, wrapping her arms around her waist and squeezing for two seconds, before she too raced to beat her cousins to the fresh bowl of biscuits Aunt May had placed on the table. It was a typical June Saturday at Southland with kids chasing each other around the house, wearing pajamas and chocolate milk mustaches.

"Mad, will you hold him for me a sec?" Jane, Danny's wife, passed Maddie a plump six-month-old boy with eyes as green as both of his parents.

"Hey, Davis, you precious package of farts and giggles." Maddie's hand absorbed the vibrations emanating from the baby's diaper as he grinned widely. "Feels good to let it all out, doesn't it?" She cuddled him closer.

Liz's son, Ethan, toddled into the room. At fifteen months old, he teetered dangerously from foot to foot, quickly developing leg muscles he'd some day use to join in the mayhem with the older kids.

Maddie knelt down, cradling Davis to her chest with one arm. "Come here, little man."

Ethan grinned and sped up his progress until he tripped over his own feet and hit the floor. Without missing a beat, he crawled at lightening speed until he reached up for Maddie. She hugged him and kissed his cheek, wondering if he confused her with Liz since they looked so much alike.

"There you are, smooch monster." Liz swept her son into her arms and kissed him like crazy all over his little face, belly, and arms while he giggled like a hyena.

Maddie stood and looked around the crowded space, missing someone. "Big Daddy, where's Mama?"

Her dad's happy expression faltered for a split second, then returned to the smile he wore almost continually. "She felt a migraine coming on last night."

It was whitewater rafting day, and Mama D and Big Daddy were supposed to babysit.

Danny sidled up next to Maddie holding his daughter, Dillon, the twin of the little one in Maddie's arms. "Do some of us need to stay behind to help with the kids?"

"What do ya think, kiddos? Can Big Daddy handle it?" He opened his arms wide, and seven of his grandkids stampeded in his direction. In the end, they were one giant group hug, jostling for positions closer to Big Daddy. "I've got it covered."

After saying farewell to the children, the adults loaded into two full-size SUVs for the two-and-a-half hour drive to the Ocoee River in Tennessee.

Mama D rushed out of the back door. "Hugs. Everyone, get out. I need hugs."

Maddie glanced at her oldest sister, Liz, who furrowed her brow and cut her eyes from Maddie to their middle sister, Katie, before she struggled out of the third row seat. She'd just crawled back there next to their surprise guest, the world famous actor Breck Stanton.

Danny co-owned a security company in Los Angeles, and he and Jane had both worked as bodyguards for Breck in the past. It was weird to see her good ole boy brother hanging out with a superstar who was also super-hot and super-sweet.

Maddie wondered if Breck might be a good match for Liz, who'd gotten to know him when she first went into hiding. But it appeared they were just friends. Not too surprising since Liz had gotten burned by a Hollywood hottie once and probably wasn't willing to go there again.

"You too, Breck." Mama D gave him the come hither hand and waited while he collapsed his long body in order to fit through the back door of the Suburban.

Maddie was concerned about her mama's agitation, since the family knew she possessed some supernatural abilities. But they didn't speak about it very often, especially not in front of company. One of the gifts was a premonition of death. With all of the worried glances they exchanged, neither Maddie nor her siblings had been brave enough to ask their mama if she'd heard the death knocks.

Once they were on the road, Heath squeezed Maddie's hand. "It'll be fine. Lots of fun. You promised." He winked.

Maddie, along with her brothers and sisters, had gone whitewater rafting almost every year since college. In fact, it was the first family activity they'd done after Maddie's attack. It had definitely given her something to think about other than Walter Braddock.

It would take approximately six hours to get down the upper and middle sections of the Ocoee. After tackling class three and four rapids most of the day, they'd be both exhilarated and exhausted.

When they arrived, their party was divided into three groups. Maddie, Heath, Danny, and Jane were all in one raft. Maddie had all the muscle in her boat, since Heath, Danny, and Jane could compete in bodybuilding competitions and win.

Look out, rapids. Here we come.

Maddie's was feeling pretty cocky until she learned it was their guide's first tour. With false bravado, Maddie braced herself for the ride, readjusting a few times. She would never say it aloud, but she'd rather have a guide who wasn't in her late teens and inexperienced.

Heath and Jane were first timers, but she and Danny were old hats, so while she should have been reasonably hopeful they would survive, a boulder of unease settled in Maddie's belly. It almost made her want to get back on the bus and go wait at the car.

As they got underway, the river churned, but Maddie's heart beat slowly and so loudly it surprised her no one else could hear it. A few successful runs over tough rapids increased her confidence, but it diminished when Heath fell out of the raft.

After the second spill Heath took in the drink, Maddie had to haul him back in the boat because Danny was on the other side, pulling Jane in.

Heath spit some water out of his mouth. "This ain't as fun as you said it would be."

"I'm sorry, sweetie." She squeezed one of his shoulders. "Did I tell you how much I like that pink toenail polish you're wearing?"

"Huh? Shit. I lost my damn shoe." He held up his naked foot and wiggled his toes as his fury faded to a smile. "Someone gave it to our baby girl for her birthday. I agreed to let her paint my toes before I realized we had no nail polish remover at the house."

"Be glad that it's me in this boat, instead of Johnny," Danny told him. "He'd rag you hard."

"It can't be any worse than what the guys at the gym said. There will come a day, Danny, when little Dillon blinks those long eyelashes at you and says in her sweet little voice, '*Daddy, can I practice on you?*' You'll cave, just like I did."

"I know you're right." Danny looked over his shoulder. "Jane, baby, be sure we have some acetone at the house, won't ya?"

"You got it, babe." Jane grinned and winked at Maddie.

The guide warned them they were approaching

one of the bigger rapids, so they all paddled hard to no avail.

They all fell out. Grinding her teeth against the biting chill of the water, Maddie was on the verge of filing a complaint with someone about their lame-ass guide. In her head, she composed a strongly worded letter as she struggled to get back into the raft.

The next time she helped pull Heath back into the boat, she turned to face the guide. "I hope you aren't operating on the assumption that the more we swim, the better we tip."

"I—I'm sorry." The guide was as wet as the rest of them. "The river's rougher today than it's been during training. I can't help it."

"It's okay, Maddie-cake." Heath patted her leg.

"No. It's not. I can't even enjoy myself for freaking hangin' on. Forgive me, I don't mean to take it out on you." She glanced over her shoulder at the guide. "Or you. I'm sorry."

The guide acknowledged her with a nod before her eyes focused downstream and widened. "Left back, right forward," the guide yelled.

They paddled and then time slowed. Heath fell backward toward Maddie. Before she could inhale, she plunged under the water. Her back hit a rock, knocking the remaining air from her lungs. Pain pierced her, and her first thought was of the spear that had pierced the side of Jesus.

Odd.

Being on the bottom of the river with Heath's massive weight on top of her, panic gripped her spine and twisted. Her muscles refused to work, and her brain clouded with dizziness.

Relax.

A voice from inside her spirit spoke to her, and she squeezed her eyes shut. Letting go of her control, she stopped struggling. The perception of serenity surrounded her. It couldn't be reality because the powerful water roiled all around her. With the exception of a few sloshing noises, it was quiet beneath the surface. She smiled when Heath got off of her, and she was weightless.

Long, white, watery arms reached out of nowhere and pulled her down. Peace settled in her heart as she descended. The strangest sensation overwhelmed her when the liquid hands began to pull and push at the same time.

After being shoved out of the water, she stood on a riverbank, looking across at a man in a white tunic. His aura glowed a brilliant white, and she squinted. He was familiar, and his countenance was inviting. She had to get closer.

"How do I cross?" she asked.

"You cannot cross, Maddie. Your work is not finished."

She looked around at the blue water, the green grass, and in the distance, a gated city which sparkled like gem stones. "But I like it here. I want to stay. How do I cross?"

The man appeared by her side suddenly. "Look."

Her gaze followed where he pointed, and she peered through a small porthole window on a cruise ship. On the other side of the glass, horses grazed near a wooded area. Three of the horses carried her kids, including Sara Ann who sat atop a beautiful, full-sized Saddlebred.

"My babies." Her hand covered her heart.

"They need you, Madelyn. You have to go back, so you can care for them. I will send the other one to you in time."

"The other one?" She turned back to the man who was again on the other side of the river.

He almost smiled. "The one you'll call Glenn."

Maddie's heart thumped against her chest, but the peace never left her.

"Go back now, child. I will see you again, when it's your time." The man pointed down the river, and that's when she noticed the hole in his hand.

***

Heath pulled Maddie onto the rocks on the bank of the river and laid her down. "Maddie Baker, wake up," he yelled.

He popped her cheeks with his fingertips, but she didn't move.

"Up to the road, Heath," Jane said from somewhere behind him.

Glancing up the steep embankment, he settled Maddie over his shoulder and started climbing. His foot slipped, and his knee hit a rock. Ignoring the pain, he gritted his teeth and prepared to keep going.

A strong hand landed on his butt and pushed. "I got you, man. Go." Danny was behind him.

He continued up until he reached the shoulder along the narrow two lane road. Laying Maddie down, he bent over her, noting the blue tinge of her complexion. He was trained in CPR and First Aid. A sharp bark of laughter escaped him because he couldn't recall the first step.

Think, dammit. Like a metal gear cog clicking into place, his brain switched on. ABC. Airway—he tilted her chin up and put his ear close to look, listen, and feel for breath. Nothing. He pinched her nose and gave two slow breaths. B for breath. C was circulation.

He pressed two fingers against her carotid artery. "No pulse."

"Let me." Jane dropped to her knees on Maddie's other side and skimmed her fingers along the bottom of Maddie's ribs, in search of the xiphoid process.

Once Jane's hands were in the correct position on Maddie's sternum, Heath reached to stop her. It was his job. He wanted to do it.

Danny gripped Heath's shoulder. "Brother, you're too strong and full of adrenalin. You'll break her ribs."

Heath leaned back on his heels. "Go," he said to Jane, his tone more forceful than he intended.

Jane began chest compressions. He ran a hand through his wet hair. If he had his patrol car, he'd have an Automated External Defibrillator to shock her heart back into rhythm.

Heath shot to his feet. "Someone call 911."

He didn't realize he'd almost stepped in front of oncoming traffic until a horn blared and Danny pulled him back.

"I'm on it." Danny held a cell phone in his hand.

Cars were slowing and stopping along the narrow road.

Heath started praying like he hadn't prayed since his mama had gotten sick. He fell to his knees by Maddie.

"Come on, Maddie-cake. You can't leave me. Open your eyes." He squeezed her hand.

"You give the breaths," Jane said to him as she pumped Maddie's heart for her.

Heath's chest burned, but he made himself keep it together and help when Jane directed him to. After what must've been an eternity, Danny pulled Heath out of the way, and an officer knelt to open an AED unit. Jane used scissors from the kit to cut away Maddie's clothes.

The first shock jerked Maddie's body off the ground and shook Heath to his core. Every muscle clenched against the flip of his stomach.

Oh, Maddie. Please. A tear slid down his cheek, and he didn't bother to wipe it away.

Two jolts later, an ambulance arrived. Maddie had described the day of her attack as the longest of her life. The last few minutes had been the longest of his. Probably only minutes had passed, but he couldn't be certain.

He rode in the ambulance and tried to keep his distance as the paramedic worked on her. After each surge of electricity, they'd get a few seconds of rhythm, but it would stop again.

At the hospital, they wouldn't let Heath stay with Maddie. He paced barefoot around the ER waiting room. Since he'd lost a shoe to the river, he'd taken off the remaining one and tossed it in the trash. He'd gladly give up all of his shoes and earthly possessions if it would bring Maddie back to him.

Praying to God, he promised to never lie, drink, cuss, or have sex until he was legally married to Maddie. Although he got the idea that in God's eyes, they were already married. It was what he believed in his heart anyway.

Danny and Jane joined him and shortly after, Liz, Johnny and his buddy, Max, Katie and her husband, Robert, Paul and his wife, Jen, and Breck Stanton arrived. They all joined hands while Paul led them in a prayer. Breck followed up with a Catholic prayer for the sick.

"I'll go to Southland to be with the kids, so Mama D and Big Daddy can come up here," Jen said.

"I'll go, too," Breck said. "I don't want to be in the way here, and I like kids, although I'm not sure how much help I'll be."

Jane ran her hands through her still damp hair. "Breck, they have an X-Box with a bunch of games, including the dance one. That'll occupy the older kids for a while."

Heath watched and listened to everything, but was unable to organize his thoughts enough to speak a complete sentence. "My dad," Heath said, his voice sounding as rough as someone who'd chain-smoked all their life.

"Mama called him." Liz put her hand on his arm. "It's okay, everybody. Aunt May and Uncle Ben Hill are there, too. The kids will be fine."

"Mark," Heath said. Though technically no

longer part of the family, the mother of Mark's children might be lying dead in the hospital emergency room. "Someone should call him."

***

Maddie took one last look at the man across the river before she turned to go. As she walked along the riverbank, movement on the other side of the water caught her attention. Fog rolled in, obscuring her view of the people there.

A man walked hand-in-hand with a woman.

Maddie recognized him. "Glenn," she called.

As the cloud parted, he stopped walking and pulled the woman to his side. "Take care of our girl." They smiled before the vapor shifted, concealing them.

"Mama."

Maddie leaned forward and blinked rapidly. A little girl across the river kept pace with her. Maddie's heart jerked in her chest again, and the motion made her stumble, but not fall. When her steps were steady, she continued walking to keep up.

Maddie tilted her head. "Do I know you?"

"We never met on earth, but I'm your daughter. And I wanted you to know I'm okay. I'm happy here. Grandpa is here too."

Behind the girl, Maddie's dad, her real dad, rested his hands on the girl's shoulders. He blew a kiss, and then they both disappeared in the fog. A gaping wound in Maddie's soul throbbed. The little girl was the child conceived when Maddie had been raped—the one she'd aborted.

Her knees went weak, and as she stumbled

again, someone caught her—carried her. Letting her head fall back, she stared up at the clear blue sky. A huge white dove flew overhead and stopped to hover over her, wings spreading from one horizon to the other. She smiled and opened her arms wide, so she could float on air, too.

Soon, she stood on her own two feet again and walked. She really wanted to stay on this peaceful riverbank, but her mind flashed to rocky borders barely containing rapids. Wondering how she'd gotten to this beautiful place, she remembered the Ocoee was also beautiful, but it had a rugged beauty—a dangerous allure.

The sound of rushing water filled her ears. Voices in the shadows ahead called her name.

Maddie turned back for a final glance. A small crowd, including Heath's mama and the first Mrs. Baker, offered farewell waves. Maddie's eyes held her little girl's gaze a second before Maddie collapsed, and the world went dark.

Chapter Twenty-nine

Heath scrubbed his hands over his face. Mentioning Mark reminded Heath of the kids, and his stomach twisted into a knot. He wondered how they'd react to the news of Maddie's accident.

Only...it hadn't been an accident. His hands shook until he tightened his fists into balls.

"Danny," Liz said. "Tell us what happened. We were down river, so we didn't see."

"It was my fault," Heath said, his eyes burning.

"No, it wasn't," Jane said.

"*I* knocked Maddie out of the boat," Heath said. "*My* weight carried her to the bottom of the river. It jarred both of us when she hit." He wrenched his hands, feeling the impact all over again.

Danny gripped Heath's shoulder. "It was the guide's fault, not yours. You wouldn't have fallen at all if she'd given the correct command. I've kayaked whitewater enough to know we should've done the opposite of what she said. She was new and got it mixed up."

"You can't blame yourself, Heath." Jane stepped close to Danny's other side.

They could say it all day long, but Heath would never forgive himself if Maddie was gone. The plastic chair he sank onto groaned under his weight. For the first time, he wished he'd never bulked up. He covered his face with his hands to hide his tears.

"Excuse me," a man's voice penetrated the relative silence. "Are you the family of Madelyn Baker?"

A white-haired man in blue scrubs moved closer to them, and Heath stood again, wiping his face with his fists.

"We're the Bakers." Danny stood next to him. "How is she?"

"She's stable, but it's critical. The good news is that her airway closed, and very little water got into her lungs, which is a miracle. The bad news is…she went without oxygen for a long time. The medics had to intubate her to get an airway."

"So, she wasn't getting the rescue breaths I gave her?" Heath asked.

"The air probably went into her stomach. But as long as the chest compressions were effective, the oxygen in her blood was being circulated. We won't know until she regains consciousness, and we're keeping her sedated because of the ventilator." The doctor cleared his throat. "You all need to be prepared for the possibility of brain damage."

***

221

Later in the evening, after Maddie was moved to the Intensive Care Unit, Heath sat with her family in the waiting room. The Bakers wanted to wait to update the kids until they knew more. They had gotten to see Maddie for a minute, but doing so sent Heath straight to the chapel.

When he was there, Big Dan sat next to Heath on the pew. "I've seen entirely too much of the inside of hospitals in the past couple of years."

Heath wiped his eyes. "I hear you, and I agree."

"They tell me you're blaming yourself. Was there anything you could have done differently?"

Heath shook his head. "Not that I can think of."

"Stop beating yourself up then. You were the one who scaled a wall of rock with my baby on your shoulder to get her the help she needed. If you hadn't done that when you did, she might not be alive right now."

"What if she's…you know?" He couldn't say it.

"We'll cross that bridge when we get there…*if* we get there." Dan swallowed audibly. "If for some reason God decides to take her on home, I want to thank you for making her so happy these last few months."

"She's got to make it, Dan." A sob caught in his throat.

Dan squeezed his shoulder, and then patted a minute, until Heath could catch his breath.

When they returned to the waiting room, Mark had arrived. His brother accompanied him, and Heath was introduced to David, who also turned out to be Mark's attorney. A haze of red shaded Heath's vision, and he cracked his knuckles.

Danny and Jane each took one of Heath's arms and gently tugged him back, until his legs ran into the edge of a chair. He glanced behind him and sat, grinding his teeth.

"Daddy," Liz said. "Mark has something he wants to tell us."

"And you need David here for this?" Dan asked, crossing his arms over his chest.

"Maddie had a Living Will," Mark said.

Heath noticed Big Dan exchange a glance with his sister-in-law, Nancy. Aunt Nancy also happened to be Maddie's legal representation. Heath's hands trembled, so he gripped his knees.

"Why do you feel the need to share this with us now?" Dan asked.

"Maddie didn't want to be kept alive artificially." Mark nodded to David who opened his briefcase.

Nancy approached and took the document from him. "Still trying to get your hands on Maddie's trust fund, aren't you, Mark?"

"This has nothing to do with that. Although, if Maddie doesn't make it, I could use that money to support our kids, since I would be raising them on my own."

"You mean with your ho of a girlfriend, don't you?" Liz asked, hands on hips.

It was a pose Heath had seen Maddie strike a million times, and one corner of his mouth tipped up.

"I'm not with her anymore," Mark said. "I

kicked her out, so I could focus on getting Maddie back."

Heath hadn't thought Mark was being honest when he'd told Maddie he sent Christy packing. It had been in response to their engagement news, so Mark had to have been scrambling for a toe hold.

Nancy closed the document folder and returned it to David. "I have a copy of this."

"I just wanted to make sure you would all be prepared to carry out Maddie's wishes should the inconceivable happen," Mark said.

Heath wanted to ram that paper down Mark's throat. *I'll show you inconceivable.* He stood, fists clenched and wished his glare would make Mark's head explode before Heath had to pummel him.

Nancy moved in front of Heath, and he blinked and looked down at his feet. Shame heated his face. How many emotions could he experience in one day? His head pounded, and he wiggled his painted pink toes for a distraction, thankful Breck had donated his flip-flops before he'd left for Southland.

Nancy placed a hand on his shoulder. "I think it would probably be okay to let you all know about some legal business Maddie had taken care of recently." She walked to her seat and opened her briefcase.

"You might want to sit back down," Dan said to Heath and patted the chair he'd just vacated.

Heath rested on the hard plastic and wrinkled his brow. "Why?" What legal business? He didn't want to think about anything, except having Maddie back in his arms.

Nancy handed Heath some papers. "Maddie

rolled much of the money in her trust fund into a trust for Sara Ann Cook."

"What?" Mark asked eyes wide.

Heath figured his eyes were just as wide, but his jaw hung open. Staring at the papers, he didn't know what he was seeing. There were lots of letters, which probably formed words Nancy would have to interpret for him. One line stood out. It had a dollar sign and lots of zeroes.

His chest squeezed, and he closed his eyes. *I just want you, Maddie.*

"Upon Maddie's death," Nancy continued, "the remaining money will roll into Jenny's and Josh's trusts, which no one can access but them, when they turn thirty years of age."

"How are they supposed to live?" David asked.

"Their dad's a successful surgeon," Liz said. "He can manage."

"Maddie wants them to get their educations and support themselves—learn the value of a dollar and hard work," Mama D said. "Just like the rest of our kids have done."

"Also," Nancy turned to Heath. "This was going to be your wedding present from Maddie, but it wasn't contingent on the wedding. It's already done."

She handed him two documents—the title to his truck and the title to his house.

"Wha—Sh—" He couldn't catch his breath.

Liz knelt in front of him. "Heath, breathe. In…" she exaggerated an inhalation, her hand rising in front of her, "out…" she pushed her hand down.

It took a few seconds, but he caught onto the

rhythm. His lungs didn't like it because his tense muscles tried to cut every breath short. After a couple shaky tries, he relaxed ever so slightly.

"What is it?" Paul asked, pointing to the papers Heath held.

"She paid off the loans on Heath's house and truck," Dan said.

Heath lifted his chin. "It's *our* house and truck, and I'd rather have Maddie than all of the houses and trucks money can buy." He passed the papers back to Nancy.

"She knows that, honey." Mama D put her arm around his shoulders. "That's why she did it. So when you two start your married lives together, it'll be a non-issue."

"I suppose she changed her will, too," Mark said. "I'll contest it. She shares kids with me, not him."

"Actually," Nancy reached into her briefcase again. "The adoption was just finalized. Maddie is Sara Ann's mom, too."

Heath began hyperventilating again, surprise constricting his lungs at how quickly the paperwork had gone through. He'd finally gotten everything he ever wanted, but she might be slipping away.

Chapter Thirty

Maddie opened her ears to the sound of a ventilator. Tubing filled her mouth and throat. As a nurse, she knew most people panicked at the choked feeling, so she willed herself to remain calm.

Someone pried her eye open and shone a bright light into it. "She's coming around. Pulse is stabilizing. Let's take her off the vent."

Maddie held as still as possible as they removed the tubing from her throat. Her gag reflex kicked in to assist them. When it was clear, she took a deep breath and opened her eyes, blinking against the bright lights.

"Can you speak?" the doctor asked.

Taking a moment, she attempted to swallow. "Throat hurts." It was all she could manage, since she was sure a cat had crawled inside her larynx and used it as a scratching post.

"That's to be expected." He leaned over her.

She forced out one more painful word.

"Heath?"

"Is he the strapping young man wearing down the linoleum in the waiting area?" The doctor's eyes crinkled at the corners.

She tried a smile, but it required too much energy.

"There are about a dozen people out there, all claim to be your family. It's a crew."

A breathy laugh escaped, and she winced.

A nurse came in the room with a bottle of viscous fluid.

The doctor nodded. "It's gonna hurt a little, but if you drink some of this, it'll coat your throat and ease the discomfort. I need to do some tests, and I need you to talk to me. Can you do that for me?"

She nodded, and the nurse raised the head of the bed.

Taking a deep breath through her nose, Maddie choked down a small cup of chalky liquid. "Mylanta?" she asked, grimacing.

"Yeah, with a small amount of topical anesthetic. Let that work for a minute. Meanwhile, can you touch your nose with your right hand?"

Maddie complied and the doctor took her through a range of tests to check for neurological damage. The vocal and recall challenges followed the physical ones.

He shoved his hands in the pockets of his lab coat. "You don't appear to have brain damage."

"I passed? What do I win?" She took it as a good sign her sense of humor was intact.

"A chance to make that giant family of yours happy." He grinned. "All the scans and

228

functionality tests look good. That's why we decided to go ahead and pull you out. You're really lucky to be alive."

"Not lucky," she corrected. "Blessed."

He nodded. "That too. I'll go let the crew know you're awake, and then I'll stand back. Heath might bowl me over to get to you."

"Yeah, he might." She blinked her dry eyes several times.

A few minutes later, Heath's arms were around her.

She reveled in his warmth, nuzzling her cheek against his chest. "Is the doctor still in one piece?"

"I might've cracked a rib when I hugged him, but he'll be fine. It sounds like you will be, too." He kissed her forehead, both eyelids, both cheeks until he reached her mouth.

With one soft press of his lips, he whispered, "I love you, Maddie-cake."

When he pulled back, his huge smile lit up his face. It didn't, however, conceal his red, swollen eyes. Maddie reached to cup his cheek. The only sight better would be the faces of her kids. Their kids.

She stroked beneath his eye with her thumb. "Heath-bar, I love you, too. Always have." Vague images fluttered in her head. "I think I had a near-death experience."

"I want to hear all about it, sweetheart. But you sound awful, and you need to rest." He tipped his head to the side and kissed her neck. "Plus, I thought your dad might tackle me to get to you first. Is it okay to tell me later?"

His thoughtfulness was one of the many things she loved about him. "You saved me."

He squeezed his eyes shut, and a tear ran down his cheek. "I'm so sorry, Maddie."

"For saving me?" She smirked and wiped his face with her fingers.

"No, crazy girl, for causing you to need saving in the first place. I'm so glad you're okay. You have no idea." He kissed her again until almost every inch of her face was covered.

"Heath, I want you to know every day how much I love you and our kids."

His grin turned sexy. "I love you too, baby mama." He rested his forehead against hers. "Nancy has the papers. She also gave me my wedding presents, and I'm so happy you're alive that I'm just going to say thank you and leave it alone." He kissed her lips lightly. "Thank you for living."

***

A few days later, Heath had one arm around Maddie while he held Sara Ann on his lap. They swung on one of the back porch swings at Southland, and a warm breeze fanned them with each forward movement.

Jenny sat on the other side of Maddie, clinging to her mama like she had since the day they brought Maddie home from the hospital. Jenny had a good reason for not letting her mama out of her sight, and it was one Heath still had trouble wrapping his head around. He believed it because he believed Maddie's NDE was real. He also never doubted what she'd told him when they were kids—that she'd seen his mama smiling down on him...after she'd been buried.

Around the time of Maddie's drowning, Mama D took a walk around Southland to burn off some nervous energy. She *had* heard the death knocks.

Jenny had gotten into an argument with her older cousin Beth and had run after Mama D to keep her company.

As they walked down the lane, they saw Maddie walking toward them. Jenny started to run, but Dixie stopped her by grabbing her arm. When Maddie got about twenty feet from them, she turned, walked into the woods, and disappeared.

Dixie heard a dove calling and looked up to see Maddie walking across the tree tops. A huge white dove soared beside her. Mama D and Jenny watched until Maddie and the dove were lost in a cloud.

Jenny went into hysterics, and Mama D nearly had too, until she remembered something her deceased father had said about doves. He also had "the gift" which seemed to pass on to someone in the next generation. The white dove was a sign Maddie would be all right. When Mama D explained they'd seen a glimpse of what Maddie was experiencing, Jenny calmed a little.

They'd gone back to the house and gathered the kids to pray for Maddie's safety. Josh had asked God for his supernatural protection. In Heath's mind, that prayer had been answered, and he'd been thanking God every other thought.

The death knocks hadn't been a mistake. Maddie had been clinically dead, but she'd come back—back to him and their children.

Heath leaned his cheek against the top of her head. "Maddie, how come you don't see the spirits anymore? Did you outgrow it?"

Maddie shrugged. "I was never scared of them until I told an older lady at church I saw her husband. She said I was seeing demons, so I asked Mama D how to turn it off."

"What did she say?"

"She told me to stop looking and being receptive to them. So I did, and they went away."

She rested her head on his chest. Scattered around them in rocking chairs, swings, and folding chairs on the back porch, the Bakers held a family jam session. Heath was so at home he didn't feel out of place for not playing an instrument. Maddie normally sang along, but her throat was still tender from the abuse it had taken.

A few of the kids, who were learning to play, tried to keep up with the adults and the tempo of the songs. The remaining youngsters played nearby in the pool. Johnny and Jane were on lifeguard duty.

"Heath-bar."

"Yeah, Maddie-cake?" He twirled some strands of her hair around his thumb.

She fingered his collar. "Liz and Danny and Jane are leaving in a few days."

"Uh-huh." He kissed her temple.

"Do you want to go ahead and get hitched while they're here?"

Heath's heart beat in his ears, and he wasn't sure he heard right. "What are you saying?"

"I want you to make an honest woman out of me." Maddie looked up and winked at him.

Heath kissed her hard and fast, interrupting the rhythm of the swing. Then he slid his daughter onto Maddie's lap and stood. Adrenaline coursed through him, and he couldn't wait for the end of the song.

"Listen up, people." His voice boomed. "It's high-time one of you Bakers became a Cook, and I intend to rectify that in a day or two." He turned to her. "Name the day, Maddie-cake."

"As soon as humanly possible. Let's say…high noon on Friday. I'll be the girl on the white horse."

"Yeehaw," Heath yelled.

"Yeehaw," Sara Ann mimicked, and all of the Bakers joined in.

They would have put a pack of wild dogs to shame with their hollering, but Heath wouldn't have it any other way.

Epilogue

Heath had never dreamed of a wedding on horseback until Big Dan suggested it. It wasn't just him and Maddie, all of the guests were on horseback too, including Sara Ann who rode Star.

They did the deed at Southland, and Liz wrote a song for the occasion. It was a slight variation on her previous songs, "Play with My Heart" and "Dance with My Heart", but with a different tune. Part of it went something like:

Ride with my heart every day and night
Hold me in your arms until we see first light
With you I soar like a dove in flight
Riding by your side, the future is bright

Heath wore a white shirt and hat with his jeans. A white eyelet dress hugged Maddie's gorgeous body to the waist, then flared a little, draping over her thighs. The hand-crafted brown leather boots he'd given her for a wedding present displayed a pair of white wings across the front and back.

Sitting astride an almost white Palomino, she looked more beautiful than ever.

The horse, a new acquisition by Big Daddy, was named Houdini because he had a knack for opening the gate and letting himself out to roam free. He was also a little spirited, but under Maddie's masterful touch, he yielded.

The party rode out to the middle pasture for the ceremony. Since Heath's dad was a Justice of the Peace, he performed the nuptials. The Bakers circled their horses around, so they could hear Maddie and Heath exchange their vows. Pride swelled in his chest when she said "I promise" and "I do".

The wild horses on Cumberland Island provided the perfect backdrop for their honeymoon as Heath claimed his wife, totally and completely.

They hadn't made love since before that fateful day on the Ocoee, and somehow, the waiting made it even better. Exploring each other again like it was the first time, they went on a ride neither of them ever wanted to end.

ABOUT THE AUTHOR

Meda White is an award-winning author who writes sweet, sultry, and southern contemporary and new adult romance. Born with Georgia clay running through her veins, she continues to enjoy the Southern lifestyle with her husband, a very spoiled Collie, and a stray cat who adopted the family. When not writing, you might find her making music, shooting zombie targets, teaching yoga, or explaining the meaning of her unusual first name.

A Note to Readers

Dear Reader,

Thank you for reading *Ride With My Heart*. I hope you enjoyed Maddie and Heath's love story. I love when couples get a second chance at romance. If you're interested in the other Southland Romances, stay tuned for a sneak peek at *Fool With My Heart*.

If you have a moment to leave an honest review, I'd really appreciate it. Not only do reviews let authors know how they're doing, they help readers find new books.

I love to hear from readers. Please look for me on my Website, Facebook, Twitter, and my Dirt Road Darlings street team. If you sign up for my Newsletter, which contains bonus material and sometimes prizes, it'll make sure you never miss a new release.

Thank you, and best wishes for a lifetime of love and laughter. Oh, and don't forget to ride like the wind every now and then.

Meda

Fool With My Heart
A Southland Romance Book 4

Lacy Goodwin crossed her fingers, hoping her old beat-up Pinto wouldn't die as it sputtered down a county road in the middle-of-nowhere Georgia. She thought she was from the sticks, but this was scary.

The property she was looking for supposedly had a big sign, so she couldn't miss it. It was also reportedly only five miles outside the little town of Willow Creek. Her odometer had broken around a hundred and seventy thousand miles, so she had no idea how far she'd driven. If banjos started playing, she'd turn around and haul ass back to North Carolina.

Ahead, a white railing caught her attention. She glanced at the printed email with the directions. Wasn't there something about a white fence? She engaged the clutch and downshifted as she slowed.

Mrs. Baker hadn't exaggerated about the sign. The letters over the entrance to Southland were probably taller than Lacy.

Turning in, she proceeded through the open gate and wound through dense woods. Hopefully, there would be a house at the end of the dirt lane. Her stomach knotted in anticipation.

If she could land this job, it would be the answer to her prayers. It might even increase her life expectancy. She needed to remember to use good grammar, so she wouldn't sound like an uneducated hick. Too bad she didn't practice more often.

Her cotton dress clung to her back because September in the South could still be hotter than hell. Not to mention the humidity. She didn't hold out much hope for her hair with her car's two by sixty air conditioning—two windows rolled down traveling at sixty miles per hour. Tendrils whipped wildly around her face, after slipping from the yellow scrunchie she'd chosen to match her dress.

When the house came into view, she took her foot off the accelerator. Her chin dropped nearly to her chest before she forced it shut. She hadn't expected the house she was applying to take care of to be so dang big.

Huge glass doors and windows looked out from the front of the log and stone structure. It was as big as the motel back home near Murphy.

Just when her lack of confidence convinced her to turn Bessie around and get the hell out of there, Bessie choked and lurched to a stop, a good forty feet from the front door.

"Crap." Lacy stood on the clutch and turned the key over, only to hear the telltale sound of Bessie laughing in her face.

"Stupid car." She smacked the wheel with the palms of her hands.

She'd *have* to go to the house now. Resting her head on the steering wheel, she let out a sigh. As long as she was here, she might as well do the interview.

Distant memories made her shiver, even in the heat of an Indian summer, but they also reminded her why she had come all this way.

Snap out of it. It's only a job. It's not life and death. With a humorless laugh, she grabbed her purse and a copy of her résumé, even though she'd already emailed it. Thank the Lord for the library and their ancient donated computers.

The car door squawked in protest after Lacy put her shoulder into it, nudging it open. Once outside, Lacy peeled her dress from the back of her legs and fanned her skirt. Judging by the reflection in the rear window, her hair was a hot mess, so she removed the scrunchie, smoothed the fly-aways, and put it up again.

She patted the faded red metal. "Oh, Bessie, why do you hate me?"

She'd have to deal with the car later. First, she had to see a lady about a job, and she hoped like the dickens she hadn't bitten off more than she could chew.

Also Available from Meda White

Play With My Heart
A Southland Romance Book 1

Southern musician and closet geek Liz Baker enjoys her quiet life. While in Los Angeles helping her brother with a house project, the simple life gets complicated when British television actor Ian Clarke walks into the picture.

Ian enjoys his celebrity status in Hollywood and is determined nothing and no one will get in the way of his plans for success on the big screen. He never counted on meeting a woman like Liz, but she's the only one who can help him with a personal problem.

Forced into close quarters where priorities and cultures clash, an intense attraction catches them both by surprise. Secrets, old lovers, and the paparazzi threaten their new dreams and a chance for love could be lost forever.

Play With My Heart **is the 2014 BTS Red Carpet Award Winner in Contemporary Romance.**

Dance With My Heart: A Southland Romance Book 2
Ride With My Heart: A Southland Romance Book 3
Fool With My Heart: A Southland Romance Book 4

Dance With My Heart
A Southland Romance Book 2

Traumatized by her past, former police officer Jane Dillon gets a new start in Los Angeles as a bodyguard. If she weren't so good at saving people, she might seek a new career. At least when she moonlights as a dance teacher, no one shoots at her. One impossible-to-please macho boss, one hunk of manly hot action hero, and one oversized Southern family set her on a course she never saw coming.

Former Navy SEAL, Danny Baker, has a lot to deal with between his dad's health, his sister's public breakup, and figuring out how to get rid of a female employee without getting a sexual discrimination suit filed against him. He's always believed it to be his duty to protect women and children, but seeing the beautiful and lethal Jane in action turns his worldview upside down. He'd almost rather go back to the jungle, except the dance floors of L.A. and the woods of Georgia are providing plenty of excitement.

If they can overcome their differences, Danny's family, and Jane's past, they might find that they make the perfect team.

Spring Fling
A Southern College Novella

Kellyn Crenshaw wants to make it to college graduation without becoming another notch on the belt of a fraternity boy. A boy exactly like Pace Samson. Forced into close proximity because their roommates are dating, Kellyn sets out to prove she's resistant to his charms.

Pace never figured himself for a one-woman man until he spends time with Kellyn. She's different, and he can't get her out of his mind. She's also aware of his reputation, and it may keep him from the one girl who makes him want to change his ways.

When Pace and Kellyn fake a fling on Spring Break to help their friends, Kellyn may discover she isn't immune to Pace after all. They'll each have to decide if what's between them is just a fling or if there's a chance their feelings are real.

Fall Rush
A Southern College Novella

Embry Harris is desperate to turn things around her senior year of college. She's determined to make more responsible choices and rid herself of the stigma plaguing her. But because of her job and the hot bartender who goads her into making impulsive decisions, it isn't going to be easy.

Stede Bennett's mission since returning from his overseas tour is to get his degree. The last thing he needs is a spoiled sorority girl distracting him. Being a Marine taught him many things, except how to handle a beautiful woman in constant need of saving.

Protecting Embry from the jerk threatening to ruin her reputation is how Stede begins to lose his heart. Being empowered by Stede's words is how Embry starts losing hers. If the schemer responsible for pushing them together gets his way, they could lose their chance for happiness.

Winter Formal
A Southern College Novella

Life is going according to plan for Sibba Douglas until she gets blackmailed. Her future dream of being a doctor is threatened unless she can help a spoiled fraternity boy do well on the MCAT.

Nash Lincoln knows he needs to settle down and focus on his studies, but academics have taken a back seat to social events, and he's coasting by on little sleep and lots of pills. The distraction of a tutor he's admired from afar isn't helping matters.

Substance abuse leads to tragedy and draws Sibba and Nash closer together. But it may also be the thing that tears them apart.

Christmas Give
A Holiday Novella

Eva Walker returns home to Georgia for the first Christmas since her husband's death. She's missed her family, but is afraid the void left by her husband will make it unbearable.

Between losing his job as an NFL defensive back and losing his wife to the star quarterback, Adam "Mack" Riggs has had a rough year. Looking for a change of pace, he visits an old college friend for Christmas.

The attraction between Eva and Adam is instant, and so is the laughter. Enjoying life again feels so good for both of them. Simple Christmas wishes unite with a shared holiday tradition, putting them on a path toward healing and acceptance. A path that could lead to a future, if only their pasts would remain where they belong.